Nobody's War

A. S. Dhavale

Copyright © 2023 by Anant S. Dhavale

All rights reserved.

This is a work of fiction. Names, characters, businesses, places, events, locales, and incidents are either the products of the author's imagination or used in a fictitious manner. Any resemblance to actual persons, living or dead, or actual events is purely coincidental.

No part(s) of this book may be reproduced in any form or by any means, digital, audio, film, electronic, mechanical, recording, non-fungible -tokens or otherwise, without the written permission of the author. For more information, contact the author at anantdhavale@gmail.com

To my wife Jaya,
and son Divyan.

Foreword

I am happy to finally hand over this story to readers. It's been a roller coaster ride with its highs and lows, but I was able to somehow stick with it.

Since this is a war story, you will see scores of characters dropping out of nowhere in a crisscross of timelines. While most of them play an important role, some also peep in to talk about how they feel about the events happening around them. Many are situated on remote planets in the universe, far apart from each other, and events happen simultaneously - and, at times, utterly randomly.

I recommend going through the character index provided at the end of this book to familiarize yourself with the people involved, before delving deep into the worlds of these fascinating beings, driven purely by their instincts.

I hope this story makes you think, question, and laugh all the same.

Here goes nothing!

A. S. Dhavale

Contents

1. Prelude ... 1
PART 1 - The Build-Up ... 3
2. The Blueprint ... 4
3. The President and the Spy ... 8
4. The Schemester ... 18
5. The Land of the Free ... 21
6. The Fought Like Kittens ... 27
7. A Mole in the Works ... 32
8. A Bolt from the Blue ... 37
9. A Call to Action ... 38
10. Oh, Those Politicians! ... 41
11. The D-Day ... 44
12. Peber's Revenge ... 56
13. Xules Hits the Jackpot ... 58
14. The Funny Crook ... 60
15. CERS Knows There Was an Incursion ... 65
16. The Make Him Take Off ... 72
17. It's a Mess ... 75

18.	Kubo's Story	81
19.	The Psychic	84
20.	Marxzib's Dilemma	89
21.	It's Business	93
22.	Ghirnot Plans for the Future	96
23.	The Syndicate	99
24.	The Riok Takes Charge	105
25.	Kubo's Journey	111
Part 2: A Storm Gathers		113
26.	Tumults of War	114
27.	Emergency is Declared	121
28.	CLAN Readies for the War	122
29.	Ghirnot Colludes with the CERS	128
30.	A War Brews	132
31.	A Standoff	138
32.	A Scandal is Out in the Open	143
33.	Matters of Confidence	149
34.	A Coup Brews	152
35.	The Chief Weighs Options	155
36.	Kimnabav 1, Ukama 0	158
37.	A New Leader is Born	160
Part Three		162
38.	How the Heroes Fall	163
39.	Damaged Goods	165

40.	Marxzib in the Middle	169
41.	Of Accountability and Betrayal	171
42.	The Fall	175
43.	An Unpleasant Decision	177
44.	Lovers Tiff	180
45.	Magnonians Enter the Fray	183
46.	The Syndicate has It's own Agenda	185
47.	Wee Ja Peepl	187
48.	Love Thy Name is Ancient, Yet True	190
49.	A Planet is Violated	196
Part 4: The Aftermath		203
50.	People Against War	204
51.	Back Channel Diplomacy	206
52.	Kubo Hikes the Trail	210
53.	Into the Village	214
54.	A Souvenir	217
55.	The Wizard is Back Online	223
56.	Jebbmy Comes Through	225
57.	A Reluctant Ceasefire	227
58.	A Fickle Thing Called Love	230
Part Five		232
59.	The Horrors of War	233
60.	A New Dawn	236
Postscript		245

Social Media	252
Appendices	253
Some Concepts	257

1
Prelude

Planet Chandrama, Neutral Zone 2. The Milky Way Galaxy.

A year after the Kill Shot.

We live in strange times, but haven't there been stranger, weirder, and more difficult times than ours?

It's the seventh millennium, and I would be lying if I told you we've figured it all out. Science has made disease obsolete, but that hasn't changed the way people behave. People are, well, basically, people. They live by greed, ambition, and an insatiable urge to overpower fellow human beings. There is no doubt that we have made significant technological advances, but has that helped us to evolve into better beings? I do not have the answer to that.

Our world is divided into two halves, the southern and the northern part of the Milky Way. Each is run by a powerful conglomerate. The CLAN controls the north, while the CERS controls the south. Several independent planet nations, unaligned to either of these, continue to exist and thrive.

Humans have populated other galaxies too, such as the neighboring Alpha Magnon and the Six Nips beyond that. This became possible because of the space attenuation principle developed by Mbe Hukowi at the cusp of the fourth millennium. While trade continues to bourgeon between these neighboring galaxies, the political dynamic between them remains unpredictable to say the least.

The Milky Way galaxy, our glorious home, is the mainstay of this un-scholarly and unverified account of some extraordinarily grim events. I, Minco Turex, shall hold your attention throughout this journey quietly. You won't even notice I am around.

The trouble started when Marxzib, a man of many talents and nebulous job descriptions, ran into some precarious intel. Unbeknownst to him, Marxzib had managed to get his President muddled up in a political quagmire. Eventually, this intel got into the hands of Xules, a small-time tradesman with a funny bone, who sold it to a war-mongering faction within the CERS. The rest, as they say, is history. This little scandal proved to be the *Murder of the Prince of Austria* incident of contemporary times. If you have read the history of the Earthen Age, you should know what I am talking about.

PART 1 - THE BUILD-UP

Two months before the kill shot.

2

The Blueprint

The Shoebox, Capital District of CLAN. Northern Milky Way.

Marxzib was buried deep in his sanbanak, the ultra-powerful descendent of the twenty first century supercomputer, breaching boundaries, he shouldn't be. He was positioned across from Kubo, meaning he'd have to walk around to see her work. Even in modern times, they worked in the same building together. President Zxea had allocated them a secluded, dingy corner that no one knew of unless they looked for it. The team had fondly nicknamed their workplace "the shoebox."

"Can you send-flow it to me? I am stuck in the Supernova B1 boundary," he replied without digging his head out.

Akan, who sat nearby, exclaimed, "Wow, boss, that's totally badass! You're tampering with the enemy's core engines!"

Marxzib chuckled, "Yeah, I'm over the small stuff. You know what I mean?"

Eager to join, Akan added, "Count me in, boss!"

All of nineteen, Akan exuded the enthusiasm that comes with youth. All ready and raring to go. *Take me with you!*

"Sure, once you learn to tie your shoelaces, noob!" Peber, who had been quiet until now, suddenly spoke up. Akan showed him the finger in response.

"Alright, enough. I'll kick you both out if you don't stop," Marxzib intervened.

He walked over to Kubo and looked at her screen. His eyes grew wide with surprise. Kubo had already breached the supernova boundary and opened the vault. Not only that, but she had also gathered a billion-plus scattered pieces of data and built them into one coherent image.

They were looking at the whole Blueprint of the CERS. It revealed every intricate detail of the northern galaxy, mainly the capital city of Jikgea. Its magnificent architecture, mines, turbines, houses of people who mattered, state buildings, banks, and army headquarters.

The Blueprint lived as a protected confidential document, not to be accessed by the public. Any unauthorized attempts to access the Blueprint were clearly illegal. Even the President of the CLAN, Zxea Qollins, couldn't have authorized such a notorious breach.

Be that as it may - this is precisely what Marxzib, and his crew did for a living. It constituted their way of doing business. Their covert operations allowed them to know things even the most powerful people had no access to. Marxzib knew the CERS better than generals, politicians, heck, even the President. Marb was a master of his trade, capable of working secretively without making any noise. The President remained unaware of most of his activities, even though he reported directly to her.

"Kubo! This is incredible. Dangerous. Beautiful!" Marxzib hugged Kubo.

Marxzib meant it more as a mentor hug, but Kubo flushed bright red after he released her.

"Yeah, I guess!" She smiled.

Akan, Peber, and Uxa all gathered around her. They kept staring at the screen with wide eyes and open mouths in sheer excitement and awe.

It took Marxzib a few minutes to come out of the frenzy before he could realize the full implications of this adventure - no, it was an incursion, that's what it was.

"Everyone, conference room now," Marxzib ordered loudly, not wanting the team to scrutinize the Blueprint any further. He led the team into the room and motioned for everyone to sit around the large table in the center.

"Kubo, fantastic work. No, scratch that; this qualifies for a much better adjective, but we cannot let this information leave this room. That clear to everybody?"

Marxzib's face turned red as he tried to hammer the significance of this discovery that held the potential to upset the galactic order. Akan and Uxa had no problems complying, Kubo did not care. She loved being immersed in her own world, writing programs that did extraordinary things.

Peber, though, had a different take. He leaned back in his chair with a scowl, shaking his head in disagreement as Marxzib spoke.

"But why, Marxzib? What's the big deal? We're sleuths; we do such things for a living, right?" Peber said, interrupting Marxzib.

He glared at Peber, "Ok, I will break this down in simple terms for you, Peber. We have breached the CERS. If the outside world knows about this - there will be consequences. It could very well be termed as an incursion - a potential act of war."

An ugly frown crossed Marxzib's face as he said this. He did not like Peber's defiance, which he thought was coming from a place of insecurity. In a way, Peber was bringing out the worst in Marxzib, an otherwise soft-spoken man of polite disposition.

"Well, in that case, maybe you should have reigned in your prodigy. No one asked us to touch any data." Peber sneered at Kubo obliquely.

"Hey, shut it now," Marxzib snapped at him. "I asked her to do it as part of the regular security cadence. She hasn't done anything on her own, alright?"

Marxzib then turned to Kubo and said, "Kubo, destroy the horse right away."

Horses, that's what they termed these code vehicles. Stallions that galloped all over the galaxy uninhibited.

"I will do as you say, Boss," Kubo threw her hands in the air.

"Why would he ask me to do something only to trash it?" She mumbled as she returned and buried herself into her sanbanak.

And that's where it ended. Kubo had downloaded the details Marxzib had asked for and then destroyed the program. Well, almost.

3

The President and the Spy

The Presidential Office, Capital District of CLAN.

Zxea Qollins had made history by becoming the President of the CLAN at the young age of twenty-nine. Born to middle-class intergalactic trader parents - descendants of erstwhile Pinopians, Qingians, and Pohiminas, Zxea had climbed the ladder of political success with her sharp mind and sound judgment. Known for her emphatic style, Zxea also had an element of shrewdness needed to survive as a politician. She had managed to keep Ghirnot Ceeth, her political bête noir - a stout man of Zwibadian and Pohminas descent, away from the metaphorical throne of leadership. Ghirnot had tried to lure Zxea to his side, using her Pohminas connection, but she was too capable a politician not to understand such provincial tactics. And besides, the racial lines were so blurred it didn't matter what percentage of someone belonged to what race.

The CLAN house had a three-way split. The moderates, led by Jebbmy Nikpoa. The Libertarians, led by Leqo Dewza. Then the Dreamarians, headed by Oklido Ima. Four years ago, the moderates had flipped the tables on the Dreamarians by electing Zxea as their president, even without having the absolute majority needed to do so. Jebbmy had shown great political acumen by forging a coalition with the Libertarians. Together with Zxea, he had managed to keep the Dreamarians at bay, despite their persistent efforts to undermine this coalition. Each of the three parties retained their fair share of rogue politicians - ruthless opportunists who would stop at nothing to achieve their goals. But none of them were as shrewd and smart as Ghirnot. Ghirnot missed the chance to become the President of the CLAN, thanks to a strongly formed feminist pressure group within the Moderates party.

After the election the enmity between President Zxea and Senator Ghirnot manifested noticeably in the day-to-day functioning of the council of ministers. Daggers were consistently drawn between the two on the most important issues. Ghirnot showed little regard for the President and her staunch loyalists. The President, in turn, made sure Ghirnot's ministry remained symbolic and lacked any useful authority. Whenever Ghirnot tried to assert control, her power brokers stopped him right in his tracks. A group of senior politicos, led by Jebbmy, silently observed this tussle from a distance. While they respected the President as the head of the conglomerate, they also sympathized with Ghirnot as a colleague and a member of the administration.

After taking office President Zxea found she had inherited a small team of analysts, led by Marxzib Lumik. The existence of this team remained a well-guarded secret. Apart from the President the only people to even know such a team existed were Zxea's closet political advisors and Senator Jebbmy. President Yirom Turox had established the team some twelve years ago to keep a tab on his enemies, both internal and external. Successive Presidents had kept using it for the most precarious issues they could not entrust others with.

Within a year of collaboration Marxzib had become an important member of the President's inner circle and had direct access to communication with the rotund office. Marxzib had proved his usefulness on multiple occasions, at times helping the President navigate the choppy waters of intra-party politics. As a result, President Zxea developed a deep trust and liking toward him. Both of them had intense chemistry when they were alone together.

Marxzib knew he was treading on romantically dangerous grounds whenever Zxea summoned him. Marxzib was married to his USC-high school sweetheart Qleqo. His marriage was going through a rough patch recently. Both of them had instances of infidelity noted in their names. Marxzib had a night of adventure during his remote planet visits with a young lady named Zeta; while Qleqo had fallen for the charms of her Physiotherapist while Marxzib was away on one of his expeditions.

Both knew of their partners' slip-ups but had kept mum. The couple's log had all entries and was generally available information for partners and other parties they had exclusively nominated.

If you must know, marriages in the seventh millennium were run by digital contracts and, as such, were annullable if both parties agreed to it. Any incidences of infidelity were automatically registered into the contracts and made available for both partners as a notification. There was no way for anyone living under the dominion of one of the two conglomerates to escape the infidelity checks. The term cheating was no longer implied in a relationship context anymore.

These laws, naturally, did not apply to the lands of the Riok, the residents of Chandrama, and a few other independent colonies. More on that later, though.

The attraction between Marxzib and Zxea was too strong and getting stronger by the day. Marxzib was in sheer awe of Zxea's political acumen. She liked his intelligence and charm. The chemistry was way too obvious.

This lingering attraction was playing on his mind when the President had called him that night.

***

As he entered, Marxzib saw her standing at the sprawling window of the Rotund Office. He was a little miffed with the number of security scans he had to go through before entering Zxea's office, the epicenter of galactic power. Her back to him reminded him of their roles.

"Kvazim President." Marxzib greeted Zxea with the usual tone of respect he had while addressing her.

"Marxzib!" Zxea turned to him, the joy of seeing a good friend too radiant on her face. "Thanks a lot for coming at this hour. You know how crazy my times are."

"It's no bother, Kvazim," he said with a sheepish smile. "I am used to doing crazy hours; it comes with the territory."

He tried to be as polite as possible, quickly glancing at her and then away.

"Excellent, how are you doing? How's the team?" The President asked as she approached him with her hand out. A pleasant, friendly handshake. He could feel the warmth in her gentle hands.

"All good, Kvazim. You seem to be busy as usual."

"Yeah, perks of the chair!" She replied with a smile. "Anyways, let me show you something I want your help on. Come here,"

She tapped on his shoulder. It was against protocol, but they were on friendly terms.

They were now looking at some pictures on a sizable Zereal screen that occupied a large portion of the northern wall. Many of the photos had long shots of what appeared to be mining operations. Then there were some in which a young Senator Ghirnot could be seen, shaking hands with some people Marxzib did not recognize. He knew this could have some political angle, but he was still determining what he was looking at.

"What am I looking at, Kvazim President?" He asked nervously.

This was the third president he had served as the security analyst. Politicians came and went, and with them went their accountability. But he knew, as a CLAN employee, he would be working here for a long time and held accountable for things that happened under his watch.

"It's what it looks like, Marb." She called him by his pet name. She did that sometimes. "It's Ghirnot, hand in glove with the Kalismow racket."

"But Kvazim," Marxzib wanted to say something but stopped midway.

She sensed his hesitation. "Please speak freely. We are friends here, Marb."

Marxzib cleared his throat and said, "From what I have read, Senator Ghirnot was acquitted of all charges back then. The reports mention he ultimately helped the CLAN eradicate Kalismow."

"Senator Ghirnot," Zxea said, "Is a deceitfully smart politician. My sources tell me he took home a good five Quantixos in this transaction. Cashed out and threw the Kalismow racket to the wolves. Came out a hero."

Marxzib did not respond right away. It was difficult for Zxea to tell whether he believed what she had told him. In reality, it did not matter what he thought; as the President, she could have easily cracked her whip and asked for the intel she wanted. But that was not her style. Marxzib was familiar with her ways as a leader, she knew how to get people do things for her, at times outside of the official chain of command.

"What are you thinking, Marxzib?" She asked him. "Listen," she continued, not waiting for an answer, "It's natural for you to think I have some personal agenda here. Believe me, I do not. Ghirnot has cheated the good people of the CLAN, and I want to bring him to justice."

She paused for a moment, "I need solid proof that will stand in a court of law."

Marxzib nodded at this and said, "Yes, Kvazim President, as a matter of fact, I may have something already to bolster this theory. I was thinking about how to advance it, though."

Zxea clearly liked where this was going, the smile she shared openly giving away her intent.

"What do you have?" She asked.

"So, during our Boxqui audits, a team member named Uxa stumbled upon a log file containing numerous transactions from a mining operation. However, we haven't been able to track down these transactions to any known entity."

"That is intriguing," she said.

"It indeed is, Kvazim President. But here is the thing that's more germane - the total value of the transaction was five Quantixos. Which theoretically vindicates your suspicion."

"Ah, that's the angle we need to work on!" Zxea said with a smile. She was finally close to finding something incriminating about Ghirnot.

"Will you look into this for me, Marb?" Zxea was back to his pet name. "And yes, this has to be done in absolute secrecy. No one should know of this, not even your team."

"Copy that. I will get cracking on this," Marxzib said. "But I have a question, if you do not mind, Kvazim President."

"Feel free to ask."

"Isn't Senator Ghirnot from your own party? Is there a specific reason you are looking into him? This could easily snowball into a scandal if someone besides us were to get a whiff of it."

"I understand the risks, Marb. But here's the deal. Ghirnot, or Senator Ghirnot as you prefer to call him, has been scheming to topple my boat for some time now. Very recently, he tried to persuade several of my ministers to revolt against me and join him in forming a new government. Unfortunately for him, some of his co-conspirators got cold feet and ratted him out to me."

She took a pause and looked at Marxzib. Zxea was a keen observer and liked to figure out what people were thinking.

"Now," she continued after a brief moment, "The senator is well within his political rights – you cannot arrest someone for trying – or being ambitious. So, this is my way of getting back at him. I cannot simply ignore this menace."

Marxzib seemed perfectly happy with the rationale provided and said, "I concur with you, Kvazim President. We must do whatever it takes to survive."

As a politician at the helm, Zxea was trying to do anything and everything to safeguard her job. But Marxzib had other concerns, which he thought were worthy of bringing about at that moment.

"I hate to say this," he said as politely as possible, trying hard not to offend her, "But I would need some legal protection to do this. I'm simply an analyst on government duty. Snooping onto a presiding minister could land me in serious trouble."

He hated to negotiate with her like this. They had an excellent working relationship, but he also knew of the dangers involved. This was a difficult ask.

The fear of an undercover job going south haunted him constantly. Politicians had a way of getting things done. What if her charm was a facade? This thing was clearly illegal. He wanted to do it with an official instruction from the President's office. Too many people in his domain had lost credibility in the past, thanks to politicians. Zxea was nearing the end of her 5-year term as the President. There was a chance she may not win again.

"Kvazim President," he cleared his throat, "Umm, is it possible for you to give me official instructions on this? This is too dangerous, even for a professional snooper like me."

"I understand, Marb," Zxea moved close to him, "But I can't trust anyone else with this. Will you do this as a favor to me?"

She placed her hand on his shoulder and looked into his wandering eyes directly.

Marxzib could not make up his mind. He found himself in a strange state - drawn to her, yet somehow unsure of everything. *Ok, I know I like her. She likes me too. But what's happening here? She is being polite about it, but this is a direct order from the President of the CLAN. Do I even have a choice here? Should I simply refuse and walk away? Am I inviting trouble?*

"I can't give you anything official. But you have my word, it will not come back to you. I have the council firmly behind me. Senator Jebbmy, too, is on board."

Marxzib looked at her and nodded his head in agreement. For some reason, he decided it was worth doing. Maybe it was the way she looked at him; something was definitely going on there. The dynamic had gotten a little charged, a little hot. It tended to become a man-woman thing at the unlikeliest of junctures. This also meant Marxzib would do what she was asking him to do.

"It will be done, Kvazim; give me a day or two. I will gather the evidence you need to indict the senator."

"Marb, thank you," she said. "I appreciate you doing this so much. Please know that my entire administration and I are very grateful for this."

"It's no bother, thank you for trusting me with this."

"You know what," Zxea's eyes lit up like she had a brilliant idea "Why don't you stay for dinner? I was about to eat."

Marxzib was hungry to his bones. It was already past his dinner time. Still, he tried to dodge the invitation simply out of courtesy.

"I don't want to impose; I had something to eat before I came here. But thank you for the offer." Marxzib replied politely, despite his heart telling him otherwise. *Accept, you fool!*

"Well, that's not going to happen, is it! You are staying for dinner. I don't like to eat alone." She led him to the dining area. "Do you like Palpanese? Zimian maybe?"

"Palpanese will be fine, thank you." Marxzib replied. After all, Palpanese was all the rage these days. Out of nowhere, this tiny planet from an obscure corner of the galaxy had gained immense popularity in the universal cuisine space. It held the optimal weather conditions required to grow hundreds of varieties of spices previously unheard of.

Zxea ordered her virtual assistant to serve dinner for two. Pretty soon, they were chomping at Palpanese noodles served with zesty sauces and savory accompaniments. She was no longer the President, and he was no longer a spy. They were two friends happily sharing tiny bits of life over delicious food.

Power was still a fugacious game; both Marxzib and Zxea were acutely aware of this more than anyone else. Zxea relished the power and the thrill that came with her role; but she knew she would need friends when all this was gone, and he knew he needed her to stay in power, for no other reason than to be close to her.

Even with both considering this, the dinner was a merry occurrence, but nothing more happened that night. So, there were no readings on the infidelity meter.

4

THE SCHEMESTER

Senator Ghirnot's office, Capital District of CLAN.

GHIRNOT WAS YELLING AT the top of his lungs. "Listen, Chaliza, I want the intel by tomorrow morning! NO EXTENSIONS!"

He cut the Vabaka line abruptly with a jerk to his neck. He was waiting for intel on some illegal hacking activity that was rumored to be happening at President Zxea's behest. He had a hunch it would somehow be related to Marxzib and his gang. He hated their guts. Chaliza, his most trusted foot-soldier, was on it.

"Listen, Jebbmy," he said as he turned to the veteran politician sitting next to him. "We need to look into this Marxzib fellow. I know he is doing some dirty work for Zxea. Once we expose him, it should be easy to overthrow Zxea and her ministry. But I cannot do it on my own. I need your blessings."

"It worries me though, Ghirnot," Jebbmy said with a grim face. He was not in favor of political sabotage. "This will leave us weak. The southerners can use this to their benefit. What if the Alpha Magnon alliance takes over?"

"How could they do that? I will never let that happen. Besides, we have good relations with the Magnonians. And even if they were to embark on such a misadventure, the conglomerate is strong enough to respond in kind."

"I am not so sure, Ghirnot," Jebbmy said with an absolute poker face. "The universe is a strange place, and humans are capable of behaving irrationally."

"Be that as it may, we have to take our chances. Aren't you tired of seconding to a rookie?" Ghirnot jerked his neck as he said this. It was a physical sign he was starting to lose his patience.

"The President was chosen by the people, Ghirnot," Jebbmy said. "Let us not forget that. I understand your political aspirations, my friend; I really do, but as the people's representatives, our job is to safeguard and respect the constitution. We owe it to the CLAN. These perks come with great responsibility. I do not want to die with the burden of not doing my job to the fullest."

Jebbmy paused as he put his hand on Ghirnot's shoulder, "There is nothing wrong with having ambition. I know what you are capable of. But there are better ways of dealing with these things. I do not support espionage."

Ghirnot huffed as he leaned back in his chair. He wanted to rebuke Jebbmy but decided against it. He could not afford to lose an ally like him. At least not now. Even though Jebbmy did not like Ghirnot's ideas, he was not one to rat. He was a senior career politician who knew these things were common in politics. People cheat and backstab. Governments are toppled like decks of cards.

"It isn't, Jebbmy. In fact, far from it. I like to call it a fact-finding mission. Let the public know how their elected executive misuses her power. And if that involves toppling the government and taking command - I don't really mind," Ghirnot responded with gusto.

"No one is above the law, Ghirnot," Jebbmy said, his face unmoved. "If President Zxea and her people are in the wrong, they will definitely be held responsible. But I need to see clear proof. I hope it's not a witch hunt you torment your staff for."

Jebbmy was in fact alluding to Ghirnot's conversation earlier with Chaliza. He suspected Ghirnot was misusing the ministry's resources for personal political gains. He had heard some rumors to that effect.

Ghirnot shrugged but did not respond. He was desperately trying to know what Marxzib was up to. A whiff of illegal spying was a reasonable size of a scandal to stir the nest. He had lost the Presidency to Zxea narrowly last time around, there was no way he was going to sit still now.

5
THE LAND OF THE FREE
The People's Nation of Priscia, Neutral Zone 4.

THE RIOK WAS MORE of a role than an individual. The people of Priscia, an independent planet nation, chose a leader every five years. They addressed the chosen one as *the Riok* and treated them with utmost respect. To the untrained eye, the criteria for selection was straightforward - they needed to have impeccable character, be a skilled warrior beyond doubt, and be an intelligent strategist. It took a lot to keep up with the expectations from the chair, and only the stronger ones could survive. Many Rioks had abdicated until now, unable to sustain the pressure.

The tradition boasted some great names in the past. Leme Kso, Roej Balvip, Syntey Grapie, and many more - each of them a unique and celebrated personality. Their legends were a part of the folklore of the land. The reigning Riok had to make way for a new individual after five years and head into retirement quietly, only to return under exceptional circumstances. Becoming a Riok thus was a great personal sacrifice. No one knew where Rioks went once they retired; they simply disappeared without a trace.

In the minds of the masses, retired Rioks had a home someplace on a far-off moon, where they lived in tranquility, the kind generally associated with the Himalayan mountains throughout the first three millennia on planet Earth. This was before the Himalayas melted entirely at the beginning of the fourth millennium, and the polar regions simply dissolved and floated away into the seas, causing the great exodus. Planet Earth still existed with select outposts and a pristine new environment that had reshaped the ecology over the course of centuries after the unfortunate events that rocked it. Humans had settled into faraway corners of the galaxies, while their previous home became a research center and a costly travel destination.

***

"They are waiting for you, master," Counselor Aeqima said as she bowed before Kinmuk Wey, the prevailing Riok. The Riok responded by bowing his head as was customary. He preferred to speak less and only when required. Kinmuk was a young man of thirty, widely revered for his knowledge of philosophy and interplanetary relations. He was a lonely soul who preferred to spend most of his time meditating on Mount Uho, the sacred Priscian peak. The mount harbored an old monastery that required an arduous trek of several miles through rough, stony terrain. Air vessels and other means of transportation were strictly prohibited in its surrounding regions.

Aeqima served as the principal counselor of the state. Her job was to counsel the Riok on various matters and protect him or her from excessively materialistic distractions. This included everything from politics, media, and the general public to any potential romantic interests. Successive Rioks and the Priscian public had consistently held her in the highest of regards. She excelled in multiple arts, sciences, and warfare, specializing in intergalactic legal affairs.

It might help at this juncture to clarify that the Priscians were not an aggregate of some obscure warring tribes; but a flourishing nation that had refused to align with either of the two powerful conglomerates, maintaining its own sovereign existence. Pihimay Veyo, the founding mother of the state, had studied the non-alignment movement that had risen on planet Earth back in the nineteenth century. She had liked that experiment for its merits. She believed the principles of non-alignment could help save the galaxy from the friction between the CERS and the CLAN. The very essence of non-alignment was to not let a select few decide the fate of the human race.

Mother Veyo did not like how the Milky Way was plundered by the mining mafia in collusion with traditionally stronger politicians from both sides. It was rare to see a leader from the weaker sections of the galaxy climbing the ladders of success. Seven thousand years of civilized history and the human race was still a hotbed of the rich and the strong. Privilege mattered still.

"We must create a third order that will stand for the rights of the weak, the unprivileged." She had said in one of her famous addresses at the one-thousandth Inter-Galactic convention. "The Milky Way, unfortunately," she had observed, "Still lags behind when it comes to equality of rights. Two absolute power blocs control the galaxy. These have collided several times in the past and may eventually lead to a much greater conflict. We refuse to align with either of these or get dragged into disputes we do not need. We stand for ourselves and our core human values of equality. We chose to lead ourselves. By deciding not to side with superpowers, we inherently protect our independence, our sovereignty, as a matter of fact, our own existence."

At the time, there were few takers for Veyo's vision. As often happens with such things, as time passed, more and more of the erstwhile independent nations under the conglomerates had grown disillusioned. Priscia managed to prosper on its own, and taking a cue from them, some fifty-five planets from the CERS and twenty-three from CLAN had eventually separated from the Conglomerates and declared their independence. Aeqima wished to see the independent planets join forces in a third alliance under the guidance of a Priscian leader, but the Rioks she worked with either weren't up to it or believed it would be a deviation from the Priscian way. The current Riok, Kinmuk, had an interesting take on this matter. "Not taking a stance at such a critical juncture of human history would mean harming the legacy of founding mother Veyo," he had reflected during one of their meetings.

These thoughts ran circles in Aeqima's head when she saw the Riok again. Today was Prisicia's eight-hundredth anniversary of independence. A proud moment in their history. The Riok was to address the people and lay down the path for the future to Prisicia's hard-working people.

***

"It is a great day today." Aeqima had said to herself, "We might be closer to creating a glorious legacy for our beautiful planet nation."

She observed from a distance as the Riok approached the golden podium. A huge roar erupted from the thousands of Priscians waiting to hear their beloved leader. He graciously accepted his people's love as he bowed before them and raised both hands, palms facing upward. Another roar erupted at this - it was that of joy, an overwhelming feeling of brotherhood and love.

"My dear Priscians. The universe bows before your resolve and intelligence today. This great land of Priscia looks at us with pride and joy. Our spiritual guide, the mighty Mount Uho, showers its affection over us from the tall heavens."

The Riok exclaimed in a cheerful and exuberant yet unwavering voice. He knew what was coming. In his mind, he had an eerie foreboding of an impending ominous war on the horizon of the Milky Way. *An enormous locust storm of fire. A harrowing howl. Destruction. Chaos. Blood. Flesh. Annihilation of the creator's finest elements. A gigantic crack through time and space.*

"I must warn you," he continued amid the tremendous uproar of applause, "Of the ever-lurking danger of wars over this majestic galaxy of ours. As citizens of this peace-loving nation of Priscia, we are tasked with securing peace and an equitable galactic order where all can co-exist and respect each other's rights. Our founding Mother," he paused and looked at the sky, "Mother Veyo foresaw what perils can befall humanity as a result of the senseless pursuit of power. As the free citizens of this sacred land, it is incumbent upon us to step up and save the galaxy from the warmongering conglomerates. But my fellow Priscians, my brothers and sisters," he paused for a moment to breathe, "We must do it through compassion and love by walking the path laid down by our benevolent ancestors. We ought to play a bigger role for the betterment of all, a shared vision of peace and prosperity."

He continued speaking for a few moments, with cheerful interruptions from his followers every now and then. It was clear how much the Priscians loved him and believed in his grander vision for humankind. Only for the second time in the history of their nation, the possibility had risen for a Priscian leader to achieve a pan-galactic stature, and the Priscians could not have been prouder.

As Priscia celebrated, two outsiders quietly observed and relayed the entire ceremony to their respective conglomerates, using their Vabakas. It was Jozji for the CERS and Ulamzor for the CLAN. They knew each other well and, in a genuine professional spirit, respected their boundaries. "We are mere messengers" was their credo. It helped keep enmity out of their unique working relationship.

6
THE FOUGHT LIKE KITTENS
The Shoebox, Capital District of CLAN.

"But we must know what we are getting into, Marxzib, don't we have a right to know?" Peber asked in his usual snarky manner.

Marxzib looked up from his sanbanak in annoyance and said, "Enough with the patronizing rants, Peber. I would not take that tone with your boss if I were you. But hey, who am I talking to here? It seems like you are the boss here, doesn't it? At least in your head, that is."

"Oh, did I offend you, boss? My apologies for questioning your unfailing judgment. That was utterly stupid of me, wasn't it – how could I forget? We are simply mindless folk, doing what you ask us to," Peber simpered, "But, and this is important, as an employee, I am within my rights to ask questions. I do not appreciate us working under the hood like thieves, skirting with galactic laws."

Marxzib's face contorted with rage. *How dare he talk to me like that in front of my team?*

Marxzib sprung from his chair in his indignation. "Listen, Peber, and I am reiterating this for you. We work for the conglomerate. We do what the President expects us to do. We don't get to ask questions. You can quit if you think it's too much to digest."

The suddenness of his reaction and his sheer anger took everyone by surprise; there was a sudden quiet and barely concealed looks cast their way.

"Oh no, not again," Uxa looked at Akan mumbling under her breath.

Akan shrugged. He knew this altercation was a long impending one. Marxzib and Peber had continuously been at each other's throats over the past few months.

Peber looked more than eager to take on his boss. He did not budge from his seat and said nonchalantly "Yeah right, the President. It's ignorant of us to think she would think twice before throwing us to the wolves."

"You are naive, Peber," Marxzib retorted. "This is a dangerous job. You knew it when you signed up. Those afraid of the consequences shouldn't waste their time here."

Peber was competent at his job, but his fierce competitiveness sparked friction within the team frequently. His behavior had taken a turn for the worse ever since Marxzib promoted Kubo as his second in command.

Peber snarled at the way Marxzib called him naïve. "If there is someone naive here, it's you, Marxzib." Peber shot back as he got up from his seat and started toward Marxzib casually, readying himself for an easy hand to hand.

They stood in front of each other, face to face.

"I know what's going on between you and the lady." Peber darted an angry look at Marxzib and continued, "She is obviously using you and you are making *us* do her dirty work. What an imbecile!"

Akan was taken aback by this latest salvo from Peber. His mouth gaped open, and he gushed. He and Uxa were furiously texting each other all this time on their Vabakas. "Wow! The boss and the President? How zip is that?"

"You are a dork, and Peber's a fool; he is sooo immature for his age," Uxa typed.

Peber had an emphatic look on his face. He knew he had delivered a fatal blow with his latest jibe. He was confrontational by nature, a master at stretching things on and on until his opponents got pissed and lost it.

Marxzib was clearly shaken by the below-the-belt attack. He fumbled for a moment and then decided in a flash it was time to take decisive action. "Ok, I have had enough of you, Peber." He bristled, "First of all, my personal life is none of your business, so stay the Zumt out of it. And second, you are fired. Deposit your keys with Kubo and leave."

Everyone was stunned by Marxzib's sudden response, especially Peber. He considered Marxzib a weak leader, incapable of making big decisions.

"Our boss lacks courage," he had vented to Kubo previously.

"He is an emotional person, Peber. He cares for people, that does not make him weak," Kubo had rebuked him in no uncertain terms.

Akan, Kubo, Uxa - all stood up in their Zerbonia cubicles. They were enjoying this little slugfest from the comfort of their chairs, but that changed when it snowballed into a real scuffle. Their office was transformed into the wild west, complete with an imminent duel.

Kubo decided to speak up. She was generally a shy person who liked to stay away from conflict. But the situation demanded intervention.

"Boss, this is a little harsh," she said. In reality, Kubo, too, was tired of Peber's incessant negativity; and yet she believed in giving chances to people.

Akan tried to say something too, but his voice was too feeble. Marxzib raised his hand, stopping Akan and Kubo from interfering further.

"You can shove off your negativity elsewhere, Peber. Your services are terminated effective immediately." Marxzib's decision was definitive.

"I don't give a Zumt, Marxzib!" Peber shouted. The smugness on his face gave way to anger and frustration. His nostrils flared out, and his hands shook. "Screw you and your shitty firm. You, weak son of a Zumt!"

Peber paused to steady his breath. He appeared to be having trouble speaking, as his voice trembled with rage. He continued, nonetheless.

"Weak!" Peber harped on the adjective, "That's what you are - a spineless fellow. Oh, and you know what? I was going to quit anyway. Good luck doing the President's dirty laundry."

"That's enough, Peber," Kubo jumped in between the two, "You are making it worse; you fool." Then she turned to Marxzib and said, "You need to calm down, boss, please!"

Akan rushed toward them too, and so did Uxa. All of a sudden, the entire crew had gathered in the middle of the room.

Marxzib and Peber were like two raging bulls trying to take on each other, partly excited as they had an audience too. People tend to aggravate conflicts in the presence of onlookers. Leave them alone and they will shake hands and leave.

But Marxzib was in no mood for reconciliation today. His face had gone red, and his lips trembled with anger. The *"weak leader"* jibe had hit him hard.

"You worthless backstabber! I did you a favor by hiring you, and this is how you pay me back! Useless prick," he yelled at the top of his lungs.

"Get out of here right now, and do not show me your face again. Get out! Get out!" Marxzib continued blurting loudly, his mouth frothing with anger.

Peber tried to respond verbally, his mouth opened and closed like a fish, but he could not speak. In the heat of that moment, it seemed he decided to deal with Marxzib the good old way. He sprung at him and swung at his face, but he completely missed, partly because his hands trembled with anger. His fist landed on a wooden board instead, zapping the skin from his knuckles.

"Shit! Shit! Shit," Peber began hyperventilating as blood rushed from his knuckles. The sight of bright red blood was too much for him to handle, and he collapsed in sheer panic.

Marxzib had swiftly ducked to save himself from Peber's raging fist, but he lost his balance in the act and went tumbling down to the floor. Kubo rushed to Peber while Akan and Uxa tended to Marxzib, who had managed to twist his weaker left knee as he fell.

"You two fight like little kittens!" The rookie Akan tried to quip smartly, attempting to ease the tension.

Everybody laughed, including a weak Peber, who was getting back on his feet with Kubo's help. Both had to be taken to the nurse's station.

And that was that of the incident.

No one reported it since both Marxzib and Peber were too embarrassed, and it mattered little to the team. They joked about it often when Marxzib wasn't around, but that was all it was to them.

Peber, though, did not get over it for a long time. In a way, he was the only aggrieved party in this affair. He had lost his job and his pride. And pride is a pricier commodity than we often realize.

7

A Mole in the Works

Senator Ghirnot's office, Capital District of CLAN.

Ghirnot sat in his chair, staring at a large screen before him. He had received a message from one of his confidants regarding a potentially disturbing development.

"Chaliza!" Ghirnot yelled without moving from his chair.

Chaliza, busy with something, was startled by the loud holler.

"What the Zumt!" he mumbled as he fumbled out of his chair.

"Yes sir, coming over," he shouted back. *Why the Zumt does he have to shout. I am hardly ten feet away from him.*

"Listen, Chaliza, there has been a problem. A few transactions from *the incident* were supposedly touched by someone recently." Ghirnot enunciated the word event deliberately. Chaliza understood. He simply nodded.

"Do you suspect anyone in particular, sir?" Chaliza asked.

"Yes. Has to be Marxzib. But I suspect he has ears here, right under our arses," Ghirnot replied, getting up from his chair. "Why don't you call in Kixmado. I want to speak with him."

"Copy that." Pretty soon, Kixmado stood before Ghirnot, patiently waiting for him to speak. Ghirnot, it seemed, was in no hurry.

"Excuse me, senator," Kixmado said, "You called me. Please let me know how I can help?"

"Help?" Ghirnot made a tut-tut sound. "How can a mole help me, Kixmado? The only way you can help me would be if you confessed to snooping around here for Zxea."

Kixmado was shaken to his core. He did not expect such a direct assault.

"That is outrageous! How dare you question my integrity, Ghirnot?" Kixmado gathered himself quickly and responded with gusto.

"It's senator, Kixmado," Chaliza interrupted, "Senator Ghirnot. We should not forget common courtesy now, shall we?"

"Courtesy? Are you both out of your minds?!" Kixmado shouted back.

Ghirnot was a little taken aback by this fire in Kixmado. He realized he had approached this the wrong way.

"Listen, Kixmado," he said, "Let us talk facts here. It was brought to my attention recently that someone from my office has been leaking information to Marxzib." He paused and got up from his chair. He slowly moved close to Kixmado, almost too close to intimidate him, looking directly into his eyes. "I need you to come clean on this. Do you get what I am saying?"

Kixmado looked down at Ghirnot, leaning into him. His face became furrowed, and his upper body grew stiff as though he was readying himself to take Ghirnot head-on. Kixmado's military training was coming in handy here. When under pressure, come back stronger.

"I am warning you, Ghirnot, back the Zumt up. I will wring your neck sideways with my bare hands."

Ghirnot was a bull, forever ready to fight, but this scared him a little. He kept looking at Kixmado without losing the intensity of his stare, but he also backed up a step.

Chaliza looked on this with his jaw open. A mundane transaction had turned ugly rather quickly. He realized he needed to intervene.

"Whoa, whoa, whoa." He managed to speak as he moved closer to the two. "Let us all take a breath here." He then squeezed Kixmado's shoulder, "There was no reason for you to raise your voice, buddy. You need not worry if you are innocent, ok. All we are saying is come clean on this."

Then he looked at his boss, "Sir, please. You need to back up a little. You are scaring the fellow."

Ghirnot looked at Chaliza. *When did he grow a pair?* But he knew Chaliza was right. All conglomerate workers were protected by solid workplace laws. They had their fierce unions backing them up, come what may. Intimidating and threatening a conglomerate employee was, in fact, a felony if proved in a court of law.

"I do not need to explain such ridiculous allegations, Chaliza. If you have evidence against me, feel free to approach the CEC. Otherwise, we are done here. You two are wasting my time."

The CEC, or the Conglomerate Employees' Court, was a legal body for managing all things related to employee disputes. It was a procedural monster known for moving utterly slowly.

Chaliza raised one eyebrow, "Listen, Kixmado, we still haven't heard you deny the allegation. Don't you think it is a little, umm, telling?"

Kixmado realized his neck was getting wet from behind. But he needed to put up a strong show.

"Haaa! I wouldn't even bother, Chaliza. Your boss is being ridiculous. Whatever charade you two got going here-" Kixmado paused, clenching his jaw, "I don't give a Zumt. But believe me, I will sue your arses if you try to squeeze me further."

Ghirnot sneered at him. "Your defiance proves you are guilty. I wanted you to man up and confess it. Now get the Zumt out of here before I throw you out to the legals."

"Do you what you gotta do, and I will return the favor, Ghirnot." Kixmado shot his finger in the air before storming out of the room.

"That did not go well, Sir. What do you want me to do?" Chaliza looked at Ghirnot.

He did not respond. Instead, he walked over the bar, and filled a large drink of the finest Zimian whiskey for himself. For a minute or so, he kept blabbering about the whiskey's color, taste, and aroma. Chaliza scratched his head. He could not understand half of the things Ghirnot had said.

Then, as if something had occurred to him, Ghirnot looked at Chaliza and said, "How long has this fellow worked for us?"

"About a year now, sir." Chaliza replied.

"Have you ever seen him come this strong at anyone in the staff?"

"No senator, never. Gets along with everyone. No complaints until now."

"Hmmm." Ghirnot put his drink down. "I wonder where his bravado comes from. Something must have happened recently."

"Umm. I don't know, senator. What do you mean?" Chaliza felt a tightness around his cheeks as he struggled to understand what his boss was on about. Ghirnot paused again for a couple of minutes. He kept looking though the deep brown layers of the whiskey in his glass. "He knows I am going down."

"Wh-what?"

"Yes. They have something on me. Those BASTARDS!" Ghirnot snapped with anger. He flung the glass of whiskey with a sideways smack. The clanking sound of the glass made him even more furious. He started throwing things around as his hands found them.

Chaliza ducked down suspecting a flurry of missiles to come swooshing in any random direction now.

"Please, please, senator, calm down." Chaliza shouted as he hid under a desk. "We can find out what's happening. Please calm down!"

But Ghirnot was not in a state to listen to anybody.

By the time Ghirnot cooled down, his office resembled a war zone. Chaliza had slipped out quietly, fearing for his life.

8
A Bolt from the Blue
The Shoebox, Capital District of CLAN.

"Hey Marb, can you meet me today? I have something you might find interesting," read a message on Marxzib's Vabaka. It was from Kixmado, his old friend from the CLANTech days.

"Sure, brother," Marxzib responded with a smiley.

He knew well who Kixmado was working with currently. No matter how hard he tried, Marxzib was not able to find anything substantial on Ghirnot. Kixmado's message to him felt like a bolt from the blue. Zxea had strategically placed Kixmado in Ghirnot's technical staff. Though he worked for the senator, his allegiance rested with Zxea. Marxzib wondered if he had something that could help the investigation. If Kixmado could somehow trace the transactions back to Ghirnot, his job was done.

9
A Call to Action
The Presidential Office, Capital District of CLAN.

Zxea stared hard at the screen. It displayed photos, documents, and several other artifacts pertaining to Senator Ghirnot. Marxzib had requested a meeting with the president to review the oppo he had gathered with the help of Kixmado.

"Looks impressive, but is this enough?" She looked at her team one by one.

Kamado served as her chief of staff, while Zebero worked as the principal political advisor. Mheilia held the portfolio of the parliamentary affairs ministry. The core team.

"I think the evidence is good enough to start a criminal inquiry," Kamado said, looking directly at Zxea then back to the evidence as if double checking.

"We would need the house's approval. You cannot investigate a senator just like that. The constitution has empowered all elected individuals with special rights." Mheilia interjected without batting an eyelid. Her knowledge of the senate's inner workings was impeccable.

Kamado did not seem happy; he had opened his mouth to speak but closed it. He could not think of a good rebuttal.

"Well, here is what I feel," Zebero came in, with his usual laid-back, almost clumsy speaking style. "Of course, this is only an opinion; you know what I mean. Eventually, it all boils down to what one thinks, doesn't it?"

"Zebero," Zxea looked at him and scowled, "Get on with it, please."

Zebero was widely respected within the senate and the administration, but he had his quirks, which sometimes annoyed people.

"Yes, Kvazim President. It will be challenging to act against Senator Ghirnot through the senate. It will be a very long process. A better option could be leaking this information to the legals and letting them take the criminal proceeding route."

Zxea nodded. *Seems like a decent plan.*

Kamado did not like this path. "That would be a weak thing to do, Kvazim President. We need to come hard on this. Take definitive action."

"How do you mean? Clarify." President Zxea asked.

"Per the provisions of Section 128C of the CLAN's constitution, the President can invoke executive power and order an arrest on an individual in question, if there is sufficient evidence pointing to a potential action of - well, treason."

Mheilia stepped in quickly, "Not the high treason act, no Kamado, that would be a drastic step. I would not advise this, Kvazim President. It would be a major scandal, completely uncalled for."

Zebero took up for Kamado playing the devil's advocate to Mheilia, "See the positive side, though. The public will love this definitive action by the President. This projects a stronger image, both to the people and our political opponents."

Mheilia scoffed, "You guys seem to have a bone to pick up with Senator Ghirnot now, too, do you?"

"What kind of a brash question is that Kvazim Mheilia?" Kamado bristled, "Going by your logic; I can say the same thing of you, can't I?"

"Take it easy, folks." President Zxea intervened. "Stop fighting."

"Kvazim President, If I may?" Mheilia persisted.

"Yes, please."

"I think we are committing a political blunder by investigating a senator from our own fold. If anything goes wrong, the administration could suffer a great deal of embarrassment."

The President did not react immediately. Her advisors were split. Mheilia had recommended a more cautious approach. On the other hand, Zebero and Kamado favored going after Ghirnot, which seemed like an aggressive yet effective ploy. A classic "gambler's call" as they called it in the capital lingo. At the time, it seemed to be the right choice for her. Zxea was a bold politician known to have climbed the echelons of power through drastic and, at times, seemingly crazy, brash decisions. Like most successful people, she did not wait for calls of action; she believed in creating them.

A make-or-break event, Zxea - you got this. She had made her decision.

She turned at Kamado and said, "Let's go the executive decision route. Schedule something with Senator Jebbmy today, I need to run this by him."

10
OH, THOSE POLITICIANS!
Undisclosed location, Capital District of CLAN.

"High treason? That's utterly outrageous?" Leqo said, talking to Kaqman in hushed tones.

Leqo and Kaqman were career politicians. They belonged to a batch of first-time senators elected some three decades ago, along with Jebbmy and Ghirnot. These four had played significant roles in the capital since then. They all had their unique brand; Jebbmy took the high road of constitutional politics, while Ghirnot aspired for power and did whatever he could to gain it. Leqo and Kaqman, though, were a different breed altogether. They prided in calling themselves power brokers who dealt with matters from behind the curtain. Their actions were sometimes perplexing, even to Jebbmy, he wondered if they were sure about it themselves.

"That's what I have heard." Kaqman replied, "The President had Ghirnot arrested last evening using her executive powers. It's unheard of. I am flabbergasted. This is indeed outrageous."

"Doesn't the President need our approval first, we as in the council of ministers?" Leqo's face became oblong with the questions that lurked in his mind.

"No, she doesn't, not for high treason. Ghirnot is a mighty chap. Zxea must have solid proof of his involvement in something dangerous. Otherwise, she wouldn't have taken such a drastic step."

Kaqman was all relaxed, his face had the glow of being in the know, "The seniors are not happy. They are worried about this becoming a precedent. At this rate, none of the ministers are safe. There is talk of an amendment in progress behind the curtain too. I am afraid the way things are structured currently - the Presidents have become too strong to fail. Ministers are - what shall I say, easily disposed of."

Leqo shook his head. "You know what, it's better than it looks. In fact, this could be an opportunity for us to eliminate Ghirnot. He knows of all our dealings in the past."

"That is precisely what I thought at first, Leqo," Kaqman said, rubbing his hands together anxiously, "But Ghirnot is a wily old fox. It will take a lot of work to get rid of him. It won't be good for us if he comes out unscathed, knowing we did nothing to help him."

"Hmmm. Let us sit this out, then; we should remain impartial and not take a stand if it comes to that." Leqo said, again with a shake of his head.

"You need to stop shaking your head, Leqo. It confuses me whether you've got something, have an idea, or are simply lost."

"Well, call it my poker face, Kaqman. A fundamental necessity of the trade," Leqo said with the utmost translucency.

Kaqman shrugged.

"Oh, by the way," Leqo tacked on quickly, as though he might forget later if he didn't say it out loud now, "I might have something on Jebbmy pretty soon. Turns out the whitehead is not so white after all." Jebbmy was fondly called the whitehead by his friends due to his silver hair.

"What do you mean, OUR Jebbmy?" Kaqman was taken aback.

"Yes, sirree, our good pal Jebbmy. I got my hands on some information pertaining to his past. But I can't give it to you unless it's concrete."

"What could it be? An affair? Gambling? Collusion with the enemy?"

"Keep guessing; I will have something soon for you, my friend." Leqo said emphatically, knowing all the power from the discussion had suddenly shifted to him.

11
The D-Day

The CLAN House, Capital District.

Jebbmy rose to address the house. His demeanor was calm, as usual. He was a remarkable man, with a sense of detachment about him. It was difficult to gauge his emotions from the outside. More of a listener than an orator, he spoke little and only when required.

Delegates throughout the northern Milky Way galaxy had crammed into the conglomerate house, a majestic structure located at the heart of the capital district. Intricate designs composed of rare elements such as Migbodium, Sterlangium, and Earthanium adorned the building. This kind of opulence did not sit well with all. Many within the CLAN, President Zxea included, thought of it as an unnecessary display of wealth and power. *"I am a socialist caught in the whirlwind of capitalist power!"* was her go-to statement when discussing social issues. But today, it would be a test of her political acumen more than her views on society and wealth in general. Zebero had assured her they had a formidable case, and so did Jeno. Somehow though, she looked concerned as she moved restlessly in her large, cushioned chair.

The house today resembled the ancient day colosseums from prehistoric times, where warriors raged against each other, aiming for the jugular. The classical Zirokjian architecture gave the building an imposing appearance, with massive marble pillars running high into an enormous dome decorated with Earthen-age mythological paintings.

A thousand warriors - or greedy little sods as Zxea liked to call them privately, occupied the rows and rows made of Diqani furniture imported from artisan planets.

Zxea sat with her party members on the left side of the hall. Zebero sat next to her, followed by other colleagues and ministers from her administration. Jebbmy occupied the tallest seat in the hall as he was presiding over the session.

"Comrades. This is a unique situation. I must say, I have not seen a high treason trial in my long career. I trust President Zxea must have had her reasons - and irrefutable, concrete evidence against our Comrade Ghirnot here, to have started this proceeding. It is up to this house now to hear both sides of the story, understand the verdict from the Legal Panel, and make an informed decision. To that effect, do I have the house's unanimous, un-objected support to conduct the trial as a facilitator?" Jebbmy asked for the house's permission to begin the proceeding.

"Aye! Aye! Yes, you do, Jebbmy." Voices erupted from the house as Jebbmy concluded his short yet clear speech.

Jebbmy was admired for his understanding of constitutional proceedings. The members trusted him for his unquestionable integrity and commitment to the conglomerate. Perhaps the only questionable chapter from his life was his brief tryst with Mera, a woman significantly younger than him. With the senator's approval, Jebbmy furthered the process.

"The trial is now in session. President Zxea, you may address the council and present your viewpoint. I request you to keep it short and precise." Jebbmy said, attempting to be impartial but clearly guarded by how he clipped his words.

He was close to both President Zxea and Senator Ghirnot on a personal level. He had known Ghirnot for a very long time. They were childhood friends who went to school together. They hung out as young men, grew up as politicians alongside each other, and shared the same circles. President Zxea was Jebbmy's student back in the day when he taught at the Academy of Political Sciences. Jebbmy had not simply witnessed her meteoric rise in politics, he had played an active part in it. Today, he did not want to seem biased toward either Zxea or Ghirnot nor did he want to stand in the way of speedy justice. As the facilitator, he was responsible for giving all parties a fair chance.

Having said this, there was a shady aspect of Ghirnot's personality that Jebbmy never felt comfortable with. He knew Ghirnot would stoop to any level to achieve his political goals. That was something unacceptable to Jebbmy.

"Members of the council," President Zxea stood up and addressed the packed house in front of her. She looked strong in the Presidential suit and donned her usual poker face. Some might say she looked pretty attractive. But today, people were more interested in learning Ghirnot's fate than focusing on the President's looks.

Outside of the forum, Marxzib and the team were watching this highly confidential trial live on their sanbanaks. This was obviously illegal and unethical, but they were hackers with good intentions, and that's what mattered. Marxzib was naturally aligned with President Zxea. His team, he was not certain of.

"Good afternoon. As elected representatives of the good people of the CLAN, it is our duty to uphold the law. Justice is not merely an abstract notion to us; it is the very basis of our constitution. It is the air in which our flags fly high and proud. And we know justice does not come easy - at times, we have to make difficult choices in our pursuit of being just - and I am fully aware that I have made an unpopular choice today, but I firmly believe in equality and fairness to all under the rule of law."

She paused as a roar of applause rose from a mixed proportion of the house. But it was also laced with the sounds of disapproval from her detractors.

"I trust your judgment, honorable members of this sacred house," Zxea's voice had conviction and a purpose, "and I promise to respect your verdict as it would be delivered."

"Justice my foot." Ghirnot scoffed under his breath.

"I shall now ask our legal counsel, Jeno, to present the case against Senator Ghirnot, on behalf of this administration."

Jebbmy nodded his head. Jeno slowly stood up from his seat. He was a bulky man in his mid-forties, well-known for his legal acumen and courtroom skills. But today, he seemed a little uneasy. He was shuffling through his notes, looking repeatedly into his sanbanak.

"Honorable members of the house. I must take you back ten years when the Kalismow racket was unearthed with the involvement of several influential traders and ministers from the government in power then."

Hushed sounds of protest were heard from some pockets of the house. "Why are they talking about this now? Wasn't that shameful chapter over a decade ago?" Many simply shook their heads.

Jebbmy knew politicians tended to have long careers, and many from the time of that incident were still serving in the house. They also tended to live full and long lives, himself included, despite the hate and scorn they received at the hands of the common folk. It was a distinct possibility that some of the co-conspirators were present, all hale and hearty in the audience. He knew it could very well have been the reason behind a few apprehensive faces in the house that had muttered protest. He looked out over the house and asked everyone to remain quiet until Jeno finished pleading his case.

"At the time, the main conspirator of the racket had not been identified. Now, thanks to the technological breakthroughs that we have had recently, our intelligence unit was able to connect the dots and identify the mastermind."

The house had gone utterly silent. One could easily hear the sound of the long breaths Jeno took in between sentences.

"This data dump here," Jeno splashed a graphic from his Vabaka on the large Zereal screen, "Provides extensive evidence of Senator Ghirnot's direct involvement with this heinous crime. The veracity of this data has been confirmed by the conglomerate's intelligence wing today. I urge honorable members to validate the evidence through their Vabakas. This here," Jeno flashed another graphic, "Is, the summarized report for your perusal."

"Shame! Shame!" Those in the gathering against Ghirnot started jeering.

"Enemy of the people!"

"Traitor!"

"Hang him!"

As was expected, Ghirnot's supporters began clamoring in his favor.

"Foul play!"

"This is a conspiracy!"

"An absolute witch hunt!"

Within moments, the CLAN's most coveted house had turned into a high street where chaos and disarray reigned. Jebbmy tried reminding the senators of the decorum, but his voice simply got drowned in the din.

Back at the office, Marxzib felt the rush of blood to his head. His role in compiling this crucial evidence had been instrumental. He was hoping it helped Zxea.

Jebbmy banged the gavel in front of him. "Quiet everyone! This kind of unruly behavior is not expected from such esteemed members of the house. Please, I urge you all to remain quiet, and observe the decorum."

His effort had a calming effect on the audience. Seizing the momentary silence, he turned to counselor Jeno and said, "Thank you, sir; you may rest your case now to allow the senators to discuss this. We may call you back if required."

"Thank you, honorable senator." Jeno bowed before the centrum and took his seat. He was clearly out of breath, in part due to the excitement around him.

Jebbmy asked Ghirnot to stand up and present his case. This surprised many; the senators expected Ghirnot's lawyer to argue on his behalf.

Ghirnot looked physically weak yet fierce in his anger. His face had gone red. There were dark circles under his eyes and his hair was disheveled. Prison could be brutal on someone like him who had never done any hard labor. He slowly got up from his seat.

"Members of the honorable house," Ghirnot spoke in a gruff voice, his words filling the air of the damp hall. "This fraud of a president," he pointed accusatively at President Zxea, "Has had me wrongfully arrested without justifiable cause or evidence. I have spent the entire past week, languishing in agony, in a high-security prison. The investigators have hounded me, not allowing me to sleep or eat properly. I have never faced such humiliation in my life. A life that I have sacrificed for the betterment of my motherland, our beautiful CLAN."

He paused and observed the house. Some made tut-tut sounds of pity. A few scoffed in amusement.

"This President," he continued, with a renewed fire in his voice, "Wants to eliminate anyone who shows the courage to stand up to her tyranny. She wants to rule the CLAN as a dictator. Do not be swayed by this political trickery, my fellow Spartans! Do not sit idle in the face of a crisis such as this. Open your eyes and look around. I want to caution you all - it's me today, but it could be any of you tomorrow. You *know* I am innocent. My lawyer will give you all the evidence you need. I am a proud patriot - I would rather die than betray my beloved conglomerate."

Ghirnot paused, and then in his trademark style, launched into a physical, almost hysterical appeal. "No, no, no!" He suddenly bellowed, thumping his chest. "I would never, ever, never- never- ever betray our beloved CLAN."

His antics had an obvious effect on the house. Many started shouting in his favor.

Jebbmy shook his head in disbelief. "Cut the drama, you fool," he mumbled under his breath.

But the house seemed to be tilting in favor of Ghirnot. He kept repeating himself, frothing at mouth, waving his hands in the air, moving and shaking his body violently amid the clamor.

"A true patriot!"

"This trial is illegal!"

"Release him now!"

Zxea did not appear intimidated despite the ruckus created by Ghirnot. She knew her enemy well enough to see through him beyond his charade. She couldn't help but smirk as she looked at the chaos in the room.

The situation had become precarious fairly quickly. Ghirnot seized the opportunity using provocation in his all too familiar style. Accusing the current President of being fraudulent was a serious charge, even for someone like Ghirnot. And he wasn't finished yet.

"This President is a despot!" He yelled. "Her minions have tampered with the evidence and misled this sacred house. This trial is a sham!" His voice had reached a crescendo as he continued shouting. His face was twisted and contorted, and he shook wildly with rage. He seemed as though he was about to have a seizure.

"Calm down, calm down, Senator," Jebbmy attempted to intervene as he stood up from his chair. He was afraid Ghirnot might faint. Worse even, he could entice the house into a coup. Jebbmy did not want any unrest in the CLAN.

"We understand you are stressed. But we must respect the rules here. Please take your seat. Now." Jebbmy nodded at Chia, Ghirnot's attorney.

The scene in the house had become extremely animated. Senators were seen talking to each other loudly, as though now was the time to speak up and be heard.

"Quite an actor, isn't he?"

"How could Jebbmy let Ghirnot speak before his attorney? Is he being lenient?" "What a scandal!"

Ghirnot did not budge, though. He kept up the act going. Chia, his young lawyer, quietly got up from her seat and walked over to him. She gently placed her hand on Ghirnot's shoulder and said, "Senator, please calm down. Let me do my job. We've got this, believe me."

Ghirnot looked at her, his eyes fuming red with fire. But somehow, the calm demeanor of Chia had a quieting effect on him. He slammed himself down in the chair begrudgingly.

Chia was a confident and successful lawyer with several accolades to her name. Getting such a high-profile case at her age was a privilege she had earned through hard work. This was a golden opportunity for her to shine, one she was not going to waste.

"Honorable members of the senate, my client was framed under false and unlawful pretenses," She got down to business right away. "I would like to refute all the evidence presented earlier as falsified. I would also like to assert that the intelligence wing was misled with fabricated data."

She then projected a file on the screen and addressed the house. "This here is all the counterevidence the justice panel needs to prove my client's innocence beyond any doubt. But before we go there - I would like for this house to squash this proceeding outright since it clearly violates Act 253 A - clause 24 of the constitution."

At this juncture, Chia paused to observe her argument's impact on the senators. Any murmurs had now subsided, and there was a pin-drop silence in the hall. Jebbmy too looked a little taken aback. He very well knew what the act implied.

"President Zxea," Chia stood up straight as she looked at the audience, knowing fully well she had their complete attention, her voice clear as day. "Is less than a year away from the end of her current term - and, as such, cannot use any of her executive powers. Imprisoning my client without a trial with an executive order was, thus, completely illegal."

Chia blurted it out in one single go – and now looked at the house emphatically. She knew her pitch was irrefutable. The constitution was ironclad and enforceable on all entities within the CLAN.

Zumt, it's all over! Counsellor Jeno thought. *How could I have missed this minor detail?* But he wasn't the only one. Even a seasoned campaigner like Jebbmy had missed it.

Zxea sat up straight in her chair, her shoulders shook with rage. *How is this possible?* She darted an angry side look at Kamado who was furiously checking something on his Vabaka. It was clear he had made an error in counting days. Gemma, the planet he hailed from, used a different date and month system than what was used by the CLAN. Clearly, he had misread the dates when filing the case.

Jebbmy took a minute to think and then addressed the house. "I agree with our young friend here. The constitution categorically prohibits the President from using their executive powers at the end year of their current term. Clearly, Senator Ghirnot's imprisonment was uncalled for and unjust. And as such, the CLAN must compensate him for his troubles. However, I see the legal Panel has reached a decision pertaining to the evidence presented against Senator Ghirnot as prosecutable. What is your decision, honorable Legal Panel?"

He looked at the large screen.

The house erupted into chaos before Jebbmy could finish. The CLAN's legal system did not have any human judges, only the legal Panels. During the proceedings, the Legal Panel analyzed the evidence and found Ghirnot guilty of espionage. The Panel was not a living entity but an advanced sanbanak skilled at analyzing pieces of evidence against thousands of simulations and providing accurate results. Its judgment was to be vetted and signed off by a jury, which in this case was the House of Senators. It was rare for a jury to overthrow a legal panel verdict except in the rarest of circumstances.

"Guilty," the Panel splashed its verdict on the screen.

Ghirnot had solicited the services of a group of conglomerate intelligence employees to plot a coup against then President Bleon. The coup had ultimately failed, but the conspirators were never caught. Marxzib, with a little bit of help from Kixmado, was able to retrieve the conversation files between Ghirnot and his co-conspirators. The legal panel gave its decision based on this evidence. Marxzib had also managed to dig out details around Ghirnot's involvement with the illegal mining operations on planet BVIOP 1. However, that was a separate offense, not a part of the current proceedings.

The verdict of the legal panel, combined with the question of the legality of this trial, split the house immediately. Half of the members favored releasing Ghirnot with a fine and suspension from the house, while the other half favored executing him for high treason.

Jebbmy decided to allow a few senators to present their viewpoints on the matter, as was the precedent. Seven senators spoke, one after the other. Three of them were pro-Ghirnot, while the rest deemed the President's actions fair.

Finally, Senator Leqo decided to stand up and speak for Ghirnot. Leqo was a career politician with a lot of friends on both sides of the power grid. Leqo had spent enough days in the crooked lanes of politics to know things could change in a jiffy.

"Respected comrades!" Leqo said, fidgeting with his hands as he spoke, "I understand the evidence against Senator Ghirnot is overwhelming. However, as counselor Chia has proved to us, the charge of high treason and his subsequent arrest is utterly unconstitutional. The President must apologize to the house for misusing her privilege. Senator Ghirnot must be released from the high-security prison, placed under house arrest, and given a fresh trial for his misdeeds. We would also like to re-appeal to the legal Panel with a fresh set of data."

The members of the house seemed amenable to this. The clamor in the hall died down significantly.

"We must not, however," Leqo continued, now in a steady voice, "Ignore Senator Ghirnot's services toward the CLAN. He has been integral to this conglomerate's progress over the past three decades. His love and patriotism for the CLAN are, in my mind, simply un-questionable. I implore each and every one of you to show mercy on him and refrain from meting out severe punishment." Leqo concluded his speech and sat down among a thunderous round of applause from the senators.

What is he even talking about? Zxea narked, not amused with Leqo's maneuver. She rose from her seat, livid with anger, and shouted, "Apologize? Never! That is not how we deal with traitors; this man is an enemy of our people. His actions have endangered the stability of the CLAN. We must continue this trial as an exception."

Jebbmy was startled at this sudden outburst. Clearly, the President had lost her cool. It was unlike Zxea. It was utterly unpresidential.

Jebbmy looked at her and said, "Kvazim President, I urge you to stick to the presidential decorum and refrain from making personal allegations."

Zxea shook her head in disbelief as she returned to her chair. Otherwise known for her composure under pressure, she looked rattled on this occasion. "This is a clusterfuck," she muttered, "A big, big mess."

She realized she had acted too hastily in imprisoning Ghirnot. One wrong decision and the tables had turned on her. This was a disaster, a political tsunami.

"Quiet! quiet please, honorable members," Jebbmy tried calming the house several times, but his voice got lost in the pandemonium. He finally thought it was prudent to adjourn the proceedings for that day.

He then signaled the security marshals to release Ghirnot. According to the CLAN's constitution, no individual could be imprisoned while an investigation was ongoing. He did not want to get muddled in any legal mess, certainly not after this fiasco.

12

Peber's Revenge

Peber's apartment, Capital District of CLAN.

Peber stayed inside his apartment all weekend and sulked. At first, he thought he wanted to crawl into dark space and never return to the capital again. But then a strong urge for exacting revenge started playing games with his mind. *This is unacceptable, such humiliation! My dignity was violated. I cannot let this slip. Marxzib must suffer for what he did.*

Uxa, Akan, and Kubo tried reaching out to him, but he kept cutting them off. He knew they would coax him into apologizing and coming back.

That he did not want to do.

Peber was a stubborn man, but this wasn't how he used to be. He grew up with well-to-do parents, both successful in their careers with the CLAN. But his father left his mom for another woman when he was twelve. His mother could not take his betrayal and slipped into a longstanding depression. These circumstances changed him forever. He grew up into an intelligent but vindictive person with trust issues.

Clang-clang-clang.

His Vabaka chimed as he tried to sleep. It was an official notification, the company sent him severance paperwork and some money per the contract stipulations. One of the contracts clearly talked about the non-disclosure of data accessed as part of the job and the consequences of non-compliance. Compliance was sanctimonious for anyone working in the intelligence community. The implications for non-compliance were both moral and otherwise. The penalties were harsh and meant the end of your career in the domain and possible jail time.

Peber found it hard to forget what he had seen on Kubo's sanbanak. With his photographic memory he was able to re-create large portions of it. The Blueprint was an important document with a lot of useful information. It certainly held the potential to make him wealthy if used correctly.

He had heard of the Syndicate and its animosity towards President Zxea. Peber also knew of the proximity Marxzib had with the president. Naturally, the Blueprint occurred to him as an excellent opportunity to undercut Marxzib. It was time to settle the score.

He looked up some shady places on his sanbanak and left a cryptic anonymous message, assuming it would get a hit from someone in the Milky Way. He was not wrong.

When you want to sell something, there is always a buyer.

13

Xules Hits the Jackpot

Planet K000-9, Neutral Zone 1.

"We need something big. I am tired of these little games."

Xules was talking to Kwaqa, his trusted lieutenant. Kwaqa knew what Xules was going on about. They had recently snuck their way into a conflict on the Planet Krita and made some cash.

"This cache is good," he looked at the numbers, "But we remain small-time hustlers. Scavengers, to be honest. Latching on to pickings that others have carelessly left behind or dropped in their sheer stupidity."

"I understand, sir," Kwaqa said, "But our reserves have recently crossed two Quantixos. That is quite an achievement by any standard."

"Well, some might feel that way, but not me, Kwaqa. I have always had great expectations." Xules smiled at his own pun.

Kwaqa chuckled, "Wasn't that a classic back in the millennia?"

"It was, indeed. I have crammed too many books in my Vabaka. More on the crime fiction side though. It helps to know the domain." Xules winked as he said *domain*.

Kwaqa was not amused this time. She was getting bored of Xules's witticisms of debatable quality.

"It's getting old, boss." She protested in a meek voice.

"Precisely my point, dear Kwaqa. Last week I accidentally overheard two influential politicos. My name was mentioned among small-time wheeler dealers. That was a little, what should I say, embarrassing. We desperately need to go big. Keep your eyes and ears open for anything significant we can lay our hands on."

"Well, now that you mention it, I found something on the dark web earlier today. Still trying to figure out what it means, though. Let me flow this over to you."

Kwaqa flashed the intel tidbit to Xules' Vabaka.

Xules looked at it closely, "Interesting. Looks like a coded message. We need someone who can decipher it. Where did this come from?"

"I found it in the dark alleys. I will check with Nizda. She can help us point to the source." Kwaqa disappeared.

Xules had a nose for a good catch when it showed up. His hustling instinct was constantly on the lookout for opportunities and this particular one looked promising. *This utterly random piece of information could turn into something big.* He hoped.

14

The Funny Crook

Planet K000-9, Neutral Zone 1.

"Come on in, my dear fellow!" Xules welcomed Peber.

Kwaqa had managed to find Peber and get him to meet Xules. She had opened up a cozy fiber globe for this meeting, as was their usual practice. The dome housed a library of antique jazz records and some exquisite Diqani furniture imported from Chandrama. It was easy to spin off these domes and the things within them. Disintegration and integration techniques had advanced rapidly in the last hundred years.

Each dome had a small space near the door, a veranda that led into a spacious drawing room. The dome could house any amenities the spinners could wish for if needed. Even a swimming pool could be easily disintegrated into free atoms and re-integrated inside. Fun and useful.

Peber smiled at Xules uneasily as he entered.

"Make yourself comfortable, my friend. Don't be scared, this is a safe spot. We are on neutral galactic grounds."

Xules was right about that. K000-9 was a secluded planet at the far end of the northern galaxy. Few travelers went that far.

Peber felt exhausted due to the aftereffect of the multiple time and space zones he had crossed within a short period of time. It had taken him an hour to travel, which was a lot by the current standards. He was surprised to see Xules and Kwaqa so bright and fresh. He wondered if they'd arrived earlier and settled in.

"Do you fancy some wine, Peber?" Kwaqa asked, "We have a rare one from the Earthen Age if you want to try it."

Peber, who had the habit of breathing loudly, nearly stopped breathing and looked up at her. He was expecting some shady, fearful arrangement. But this was turning out to be completely opposite. A little classy too.

"I don't know, well, thank you, but I'll pass," Peber said as he looked around. The globe was neatly decorated with vintage wooden furniture. A Thelonious Monk album played in the background. He also noticed a collection of paper books.

Xules could clearly see the beads of sweat on his forehead. He put a hand on Peber's shoulder to reassure him. "Relax, my fellow. Tell us what you have, and we will take good care of you."

Take good care of you? What the Zumt! Peber was scared.

"What do you mean by that?" Peber looked at Xules, gauging the man like prey with a predator.

"I can get you placed in a high position within the CERS. It's a progressive entity, nothing clammy like the CLAN; they welcome all talent with open arms, especially if they come through me. Imagine having your own crew, the leadership role that you wanted forever. And yes, let us remember the cash component that Kwaqa must have spoken with you about."

Kwaqa nodded in agreement. The number was indeed impressive. Peber could never have imagined making that much money.

Xules had obviously done his homework. He knew well what people truly wanted in life - which was to have control. Control that satisfied their fragile egos. No wonder he had tapped right into Peber's ego with the leadership offer.

"Well," Peber wiped the sweat on his forehead with his palms and then onto his sleeves.

Kwaqa cringed and made a gagging motion behind his back. "Gross!" she grumbled.

"So, there's this smart girl in Marxzib's team; her name's Kubo." He started talking, "She broke into the CERS's defense and got her hands on their Blueprint."

Xules was listening intently. He had some faint idea it was important, but he did not understand what the Blueprint was or what its significance was.

"What's this Blueprint about?" Kwaqa jumped in before Xules. Xules was not amused but got into the flow anyways.

"It's a structural diagram of all their important buildings, safety installations, and key infrastructure. If there was a war tomorrow and the CLAN had this information, they could crush the CERS easily." Peber paused and then continued, all while maintaining strong eye contact with Xules, "It's akin to opening up the sanctum sanctorum to the enemy."

Xules's eyes grew wide. He looked at Kwaqa for a moment. *This is big - way bigger than we initially thought.* Kwaqa gleaned his meaning from the familiar look.

"And you have this diagram, the Blueprint, with you?" He asked hastily.

"No, I am afraid I do not. But I have been able to draw a miniature copy of it from my memory. With my photographic memory, that is," Peber replied.

"Photographic memory." Kwaqa scoffed, "Uh, I don't know about that. It sounds like a tall claim."

"Well, try me. You can show me any picture for a second or two. I should be able to describe it in minute detail for you," Peber said firmly.

"Ok," Kwaqa replied before Xules could say anything, "Why don't you close your eyes and describe this dome back to us?"

"Is that necessary, Kwaqa?" Xules narrowed his eyes, giving her a questioning look. For some reason, he had found Peber's story entirely believable.

"Well, we have some free time on our hands, boss," she said, "And it won't hurt to validate, I guess?"

"Ok," Xules said. He trusted Kwaqa's judgment. "But remember, you found him,"

Peber did not like Xules talking about him like he wasn't in the room.

"Excuse me. I am sitting here, right in front of you. I do not like people addressing me in the third person like I don't exist." he said indignantly. Then he looked at Kwaqa and said, "You've got a deal; tell me when to start."

"Your time starts now," she replied.

"Ok, here you go," Peber closed his eyes and started talking, "A transparent Polyzcerkonium Qoxide dome, about two thousand square feet in size. Two doors, two windows. I can see the expansive prairies on the outside. A row of Bur-oaks right next to us. A large Mahogany bookshelf is on the right, with approximately four hundred old-style books. A series of Shakespeare. Also seen are Dante, William Carlos Williams, Eliot, Gibran, and some Urdu books. Probably a deewan of Meer Taqui Meer. On the left is an extensive collection of nineteenth-century Jazz Music. Monk, Armstrong, Davies. A blues record by Blind Blake."

"That's alright, we get the point," Xules interrupted Peber.

Kwaqa looked at Xules emphatically. It was her "I told you so!" look.

"I get it, Kwaqa, a good find. Do you really have to boast about it?" He half complained.

"Anyways," Peber boasted then, "The part I have drawn is good enough for an enemy state to use as a "bargaining chip" or whatever you politicians call it."

"I am not a politician, please!" Xules sneered. "Oh god, call me an agent or a hustler; I don't mind, but ugh, not a politician."

"Oh no, yeah, I mean they are our customers, ok, alright, I guess anything goes, but not a politician," Kwaqa said.

"Despicable. Atrocious!" Xules reacted.

"Abominable!" Kwaqa jumped right back in.

Peber could not resist smiling. *These crooks are fun.* He felt at ease with them and flowed over the Blueprint to Xules.

The whole transaction was over within a few minutes. As a favor, Xules gave Peber a shot of Xozilamide Acetate to relieve his space lag. And a few extra-complimentary puns that Peber failed to find remotely funny.

15
CERS KNOWS THERE WAS AN INCURSION
Planet K000-9, Neutral Zone 1.

XULES WAS DELIGHTED AT their discovery. He decided to stay put on K000-9 for a bit until he got through completely with the tidbit of information. Kwaqa had spun off a cozy little place for them to stay put for a while, so there was no rush.

K000-9 was in a far remote corner of the Milky Way. There was something known as the great void beyond the planet until the next galaxy. Zillions of light years of nothingness. In the past, crossing the great void was a dangerous endeavor only performed under unique circumstances. People preferred taking alternate routes to visit neighboring galaxies.

The human population was scattered throughout the Milky Way and beyond. People occupied places as they found them suitable to support their endeavors. The Milky Way is a large place with billions of planets. But the population was centered on a handful of livable planets. Depending on their shapes, sizes and other factors, the planets were sometimes referred to as Qanets, Finets and X-Lands. People preferred giant terrestrial planets for larger colonies. However, the obscure habitable smaller planets weren't completely ignored either.

There were always some off-gridders to be found staying in some quiet nook. These planets were also a favorite with space hikers, monks and meditators.

Kwaqa knew that K000-9 had a monastery and her sanbanak had noted several hikers on the opposite side of the planet. Other than that, the planet appeared to be secluded enough for their deliberations. Kwaqa had invited representatives from the CERS for a small conference under the pretense of light metal explorations. She knew it was difficult to get CERS folks out there otherwise. Nobody enjoyed the space lag from such a long trip. She'd ordered enough vials of Xozilamide Acetate for their guests to make them comfortable after they arrived. Even at the tender age of twenty, Kwaqa had learned the intricate ways of dealing with politicians and businesspeople.

"Our guests should be here any minute now," she informed Xules, "Have you decided how to break the news to them? They will be shocked and might get offended."

"Well, it shall be delivered with the famous *"Xulesean"* charm, Kwaqa," Xules quipped calmly. "I am confident the delegation would find it amusing that their arch-rival has almost made it to their sanctum sanctorum."

"I get it, boss. But what's with the Zen voice?"

"It's a package, Kwaqa. We are business folk. We must come across as credible."

"And the voice helps how?" Kwaqa rolled her eyes.

"Not the eye roll, Kwaqa. That is a high school thing from the Earthen Age."

Both laughed.

Kwaqa's Vabaka told her the guests had arrived. She got up from her comfy chair and signaled Xules.

The delegation appeared from the light mist that was created around travelers.

Xules welcomed them with an emphatic smile.

"Chief Lieutenant Lopki and the wise General Nodfi! It's a pleasure to host you here."

"Xules, my old friend, I am slightly perplexed. Why should you invite us to this godforsaken place." Lopki said with a hint of irritation in his husky voice.

Xules let out a hearty laugh, the one that was often seen in English movies from the nineteen sixties.

"Well, the matter is such that it couldn't have been handled anywhere else."

"Understood," Lopki said, "Now, let's get on with it. General Nodfi here is busy, and so am I."

"So, what's this deal with the light metals? Have you learned something that we do not know already?" The general jumped straight in and fired at Xules. The man had little patience.

"My sincerest apologies, honorable General." Xules tried to be as polite as possible. His face looked funny when he tried to do that, with crinkled eyes and a wide false grin.

Kwaqa called it his cheesy face. For her, the expression was invariably too much, a little less believable.

"It is a critical matter that pertains to the safety and security of the CERS. I needed some excuse to invite you this far out."

"Safety of the CERS?" Lopki sneered, "What would you have to do with it, my dear Xules? You were a businessman last I heard."

"Precisely, Chief Lieutenant Lopki. But a businessman needs to have his eyes and ears open all the time; you never know what will jump at you!"

Xules attempted to hop as he spoke. He could hardly move, thanks to the wine he had been sipping the whole afternoon, so it ended up being a skip of sorts.

"Enough with the histrionics, Xules! Out with it now," Lopki waved his hand impatiently in front of him.

"So, this is how the story goes." Xules was obviously going to take his time. Kwaqa looked away and sort of half laughed. She felt relieved someone else was being subjected to this irritating habit of his for a change.

"As you are well aware," he looked up at the towering general, "President Zxea runs a covert intelligence operation under Marxzib Lumik. Its sole purpose is to conduct illegal hacking and gather input to help Zxea make strategic decisions. We have come to know that this time around, Marxzib and his team were able to breach the T13 perimeter and steal a critical document."

"The T13 Perimeter?" General Nodfi's voice went up several notches. "How on Earth would you know about it? Anyways, I think you are jesting - it's impossible to breach the perimeter. Whoever's telling you these things is wrong."

"The fact that I know of the perimeter, hitherto a closely guarded secret, bears testimony to the authenticity of my intel," Xules replied.

"He did not actually say *hitherto*, did he?" Kwaqa mumbled.

"Hitherto? What on Zumt does that mean?" Lopki asked.

"Up until now, it's an archaic term." The general's face twisted with displeasure, "Get on with it, Xules."

"Precisely. And by the way, I like how you replaced Earth with Zumt in that expression." Xules threw his chin a bit up and raised one of his eyebrows. This was his peculiar way of telling someone he was enjoying the conversation.

"So anyways, the long and the short of it is this - a small team of analysts working directly for the President of the CLAN managed to breach your defenses and download the entire CERS Blueprint, which was subsequently destroyed."

Xules blurted out the whole thing in one breath. He had, on purpose, not told them the entire thing. The part that Xules left out was this - *it was an unauthorized breach, not endorsed by the President of the CLAN.*

For a minute, Kwaqa's globe went dead silent. The general and Lopki did not know how to react to this. It was their worst nightmare made real.

"But how could-? I mean, it's imposs- isn't it, General?" Lopki appeared utterly befuddled. He couldn't believe any part of the CERS was breachable.

The general had by now recovered and asked the obvious question. "How do I know you are not messing with us, Xules? First, the perimeter has traditionally been considered impenetrable. Secondly, even if someone managed to breach it, the Blueprint does not exist as a unified single entity. It's scattered across scores of sanbanaks. It would take someone years to assemble it as a single artifact."

"Thank you, General," Xules said emphatically, "For asking that question. I have an abstract version; you can see it and verify if it's genuine. That, of course, comes with a price. I understand this is a question of galactic security, a precious one." Xules knew he was in neutral territory; CERS had no jurisdiction here to force his hand for the intel.

"You will get your price, Xules. What do you want?"

Xules knew the general was good for his word. But he wanted something on top of currency.

"A seat at the intragalactic board of trades, my revered General," Xules grinned broadly before adding icing to the cake because that was not all he wanted, "And I want the CERS to expunge any *aberrations* it has on me."

"Don't be greedy, Xules." The general growled. He did not like negotiating with crooks.

"What do you mean by aberrations, Xules?" Lopki asked.

"Petty crimes are what they are if you ask me." The general growled once more.

Xules preferred to not look at either of them, pretending he did not hear that part.

"Listen, Xules," the general turned to Xules, "I will try, but I cannot promise anything. I will have to check with the legal folk".

"That is all I want, General!" Xules put his hand on the general's shoulder giving it a squeeze at his success. The general gave him an oblique eye.

"Oh, and yes, let us remember the cash component of the price." Kwaqa chimed in. She knew Xules could get carried away. It was her job to intervene when necessary.

"Ok. Cash would be pretty straightforward, but I must see the asset first." The general demanded.

Xules flowed the artifact through his Vabaka to both the lieutenant and the general. Peber's depiction was reasonably good enough for the CERS officers to be convinced that their defense was indeed compromised.

"This is an act of war!" The general shouted before heading for the exit, "Lopki, we need to appraise the security council immediately. The CLAN has crossed a boundary this time. They must be met with a befitting reply."

Both of them left in a jiffy.

"Our job here is done, Kwaqa, now is the time to enjoy the fruit of our hard labor."

"You are dead right, Mr. Kamperts. I have arranged for some Palpanese food. I guess we can have it now!"

"We must, my dear Kwaqa. Who knows when this war shall end!"

Both had a hearty laugh. For them, every conflict was an opportunity. A full-fledged war was a gold mine.

16

The Make Him Take Off

A plush suburb on the outskirts of the Capital District of CLAN.

As they waited for security to let them in, Kaqman said to Leqo, "It seems like we have wasted our lives." He was obviously referring to Ghirnot's wealth.

Ghirnot had accumulated a vast fortune over the years. He lived in a rich neighborhood outside the capital in a stately mansion. It was an altered Chizrobian home with a magnificent glass facade surrounded by a sprawling garden, filled with exotic flower species from every corner of the galaxy.

"Indeed, my friend," said Leqo, "Ghirnot has used his position well. I don't know where he gets his money from or how he avoids paying taxes, but this is unbelievable," he said, pointing at the mansion. "Easily the wealthiest of us all."

"Yes. Clever little fox he is," Kaqman said. "From what I have heard, much of his wealth comes from the mining operations over BVIOP."

Pretty soon, they found themselves waiting in a massive hall. The butler sat them on a rare Plikorian wood couch, easily the most expensive piece of furniture in that part of the galaxy. Leqo caught Kaqman observing the minutiae of the house, the antiques, and the overflow of riches that adorned it.

"It's pointless, Kaqman, this vulgar show of wealth," he remarked, "Ghirnot will languish in some faraway cell for a long time if Zxea has her way. Wealth does little to cure us of our flaws."

"Ain't that the truth," Kaqman mumbled as he continued evaluating their surroundings.

"Look who we have here. My friend of forty years who plainly asked the jury to place me under house arrest," Ghirnot said as he entered the drawing room. He looked a little tired but fierce as usual in an expensive-looking Earthen Age kimono, with large, unmissable Migbodium coated buttons along the side.

"I was only trying to save you, Ghirnot. You know it," Leqo responded. "Did they put the chip on you?"

"Yes, they sure as Zumt did," Ghirnot held up his hand to show a tiny chip embedded on his wrist. It was to stop him from stepping outside his house until the investigation was over. "Anyways, what would you gentlemen like to have? I have some rare scotch from the old days." Ghirnot tried to be a good host.

"We are good, Senator, thank you," Kaqman said, "We are here to discuss something important."

"Go on then," Ghirnot replied as he relaxed into a massive recliner.

"You need to leave, run away," Leqo wasted no time getting to it. "The evidence against you is overwhelming. For now, we have somehow managed to stall the proceedings, but we both know that is not a permanent solution, my friend,"

"I am not a coward, Leqo. I will perish fighting but never run." Ghirnot thundered.

"I understand you are angry, Ghirnot, but stay with me. What do you think is going to happen next time during the trial? How will you get out of this unless your lawyers can prove otherwise?" Leqo said, taking pauses and nodding in-between.

"Listen, Leqo, Kaqman. I understand you are trying to help," Ghirnot's face puckered. "But this could backfire easily. It's not difficult to find a man on the run these days."

"You don't have to worry about that," Kaqman said. "We have made arrangements. You will be safe from Zxea's people. No one would know where you are."

"Yes. Take this opportunity and hunker down for a while. Who knows what will happen next? We may have a new government at the helm soon. We will get you back as soon as conditions become favorable," Leqo asserted.

Ghirnot did not respond right away. He leaned further back into his plush chair, crossing one leg over the other. He did not like the position he was in. He was getting squeezed into a corner for the first time in his long political career.

"Let me think about this, OK," he said after a moment or two. "I understand you must have some motive but let me ask this anyways. What's in it for you?" It was more or less a rhetorical question.

"No agenda - we are only looking out for a needy friend here. Let us know your thoughts by tomorrow; we don't have much time." Kaqman said as he got up to shake Ghirnot's hand.

Ghirnot did not reciprocate. He simply looked away.

"What an arrogant son of a gun, literally snubbed me," Kaqman said on their way out.

"Well, you don't expect civility from politicians, do you? What are you - a good person?" Leqo remarked.

17
IT'S A MESS
The Presidential Office, Capital District of CLAN.

Zxea sat in the large imposing Presidential chair behind a designer Woxbi table. Standing across from her, on the right, was Kamado. Marxzib and Zebero occupied two chairs on the left. Kamado liked to stand all the time. It was his style.

"I need the truth, the whole truth. And I need it now," Zxea was clearly flustered. Her hair was disheveled, and she didn't exactly look as attractive as she usually did. Marxzib still felt attracted to her. A sign of a man hopelessly in love.

"Kvazim President, it all happened as part of our scans through the milky way. These scans happen all the time as part of our vigilance protocol," Marxzib explained. "I had asked my team to probe the possibility of breaching the B1 perimeter per the diktat we received from the Conglomerate Risk Group a while back. They wanted to know if such a possibility existed in case of an unprovoked attack by the CERS."

Zxea leaned forward in her chair toward the massive table before her. It was an impressive piece of furniture with polished surfaces and beautiful curves. She rested her elbows on the table and rubbed her hands together. All the while, her gaze was fixed on a massive Symbolist painting on the wall. The picture had survived five thousand years and still looked majestic.

A few moments passed like this. The team observed the President watchfully. Kamado looked at Marxzib; he, in turn, looked at Zebero.

"Ahem," Zebero cleared his throat and said, "I am aware of this diktat in question, Kvazim President," Zebero spoke like he was walking on eggshells with his voice. It was not unusual for him, no matter the situation. "I am sure the CERS must be running similar scans in our regions too. These are standard risk protocols. Everybody follows them."

Zxea got up from her seat, pacing up and down the room. The brooding from a few moments ago had now given way to impatience. "Ok, so what went wrong?"

"One of my new recruits, Kubo, you may remember as the smart one from the team, breached the perimeter and was able to consolidate the CERS's blueprint from thousands of scattered elements." Marxzib spoke slowly, in a low voice, apparently trying to control the damage. But the slow shuffle of his hands and the wrinkles on his forehead weakened his attempt.

Kamado raised his eyebrows in disbelief, "Marxzib, I don't believe this was an accident. She may not have had wrong intentions, but this looks like a deliberate attempt to me. Maybe she was trying to test one of her programs or to show you how brilliant she is. Talented people tend to seek validation at times."

"What makes you think this was a deliberate attempt, Kamado?" Zebero spoke for the first time. He naturally had a soft corner for Marxzib. "We ran a background check on young Kubo. She is clean as a whistle. And she is smart."

"The CERS Blueprint does not exist as a single entity," Kamado replied in the same calm voice. "For security reasons, it exists scattered, assembled only when needed. Kubo must have run another program to consolidate the image from thousands of sanbanaks spread throughout the CERS. I fail to see how we can demonstrate this was not a deliberate attempt. Also, I haven't heard Marxzib confirming whether this was an explicit ask from him or the Conglomerate Risks Group."

"Ok, I get it," Zebero jumped in. "Marxzib, is it possible for you to provide evidence that Kubo found this Blueprint in question, consolidated and ready, on one of their exterior sanbanaks?"

"And how is this supposed to help us?" Kamado interrupted.

"Well, technically, if she found the file in its entirety on an exterior neutral system as part of our daily audits, it would basically mean she did not breach the perimeter. It was an accident. Perhaps we could also say it was a security lapse, an oversight on the part of the CLAN. This will buy us enough time to negotiate and potentially de-escalate the situation."

"Sounds wacky – though strangely plausible enough to me," Zxea said as she turned to Marxzib, "Is this something you could do?"

"I believe it's possible, speaking theoretically. I mean, we could potentially - and I am thinking out loud here - plant an image there and pretend we merely stumbled upon it. Wipe off the timestamps." Marxzib scratched his head.

"You don't sound all too confident to me. Do I see a but coming, Marxzib?" Zxea was irked.

"Well, umm. Pfft." The scratching continued, this time with a furrowed forehead.

"Spit it out, Marxzib!" Zebero edged him along.

"Well, in my sheer panic, I had asked Kubo to destroy the vehicle right after. She will have to work on it again, create the Blueprint and plant it in the neutral zone."

"It still sounds risky and silly," Kamado said.

Zebero narrowed his eyes and turned to Kamado, "I will ignore the silly part, but risky? How?" Kamado's usual bluntness irritated him.

"Let us say she can reconstruct it," Kamado continued, "Considering she was the one who created it, and if she is indeed as smart as you proclaim - wouldn't the CERS detect it on their radars? Especially now, when eyes and ears are wide open everywhere."

Kamado was right. Marxzib simply shook his head. "I will see what I can do. There are ways to do these things cleverly and hide our tracks."

Marxzib bowed to the President to signal his leave of the room. He'd been fidgeting in his seat, uncomfortable with the rising heat on him.

"But wait, Marxzib. That's only half of it - how did the CERS know of the breach? Either they detected it on their own, which I highly doubt, or someone ratted us out. The question is, who was it?"

Kamado did not want to let this slip easily. It was partly his job to get the facts right for the President, but for the most part, he enjoyed pissing people off by asking questions.

"It must have been Xules if I were to take a guess," Marxzib was quick to cite Xules. "He is the only person with his claws burrowed deep in both the CLAN and the CERS."

"That sounds perfectly logical to me," Zxea said. "But how did the information reach Xules? Do you suspect anyone from your team?"

Marxzib strongly suspected that Peber may have acted out of anger. But he had no proof of Peber's involvement. Yet.

"Listen folks, I do not have any solid evidence but a hunch. It could have been Peber, an ex-analyst from my team. He was fired for disciplinary reasons from the unit a while ago. He might have had access to a part of the Blueprint."

"A part of it? Did he have a version of it?" Kamado jumped to the offensive, his posture somehow becoming ramrod straight.

"No, no one had the Blueprint except Kubo, not even me. But the guy has a photographic memory. He could have easily created a partial view of it."

"Hmmm." Zxea let out a huge sigh. *This thing keeps getting more complicated by the minute. How do I stop this juggernaut, ready to roll all over us?*

"Listen, everyone," she spoke sternly, "I want you all to work together, and find a way out of this mess. I need a compelling story to pitch to these idiots before I can approach the CERS."

Zxea stormed out of the room taking with her the last word.

By "*idiots,*" she'd been referring to the CSC, the CLAN security council. The council disapproved of the President's recent activities and was inclined to concur with the increasing perception that the President had become overly ambitious and reckless. Ghirnot's departure from the administration meant that the CLAN lacked a potent opposition that could hold the President in check. Zxea feared that the council would instigate a no confidence motion against her. Her illustrious career would essentially come to an end if this happened. No President in the recent history of the CLAN had survived a no confidence motion. The odds were clearly against her.

Kamado followed her with the usual smugness on his face. He had a leg up in the President's inner circle now. Marxzib had obviously screwed up. Kamado knew the President would not be able to protect Marxzib this time, even if she wanted to. He suspected something was going on between the two. He secretly liked Zxea; but she never allowed the wall between them to break. Zxea was fierce when required, she had mastered the art of keeping her staff at arm's length. She avoided any interest in their personal matters. This was a deliberate, political choice. A power play.

Zebero was split with mixed feelings. He was a kind soul and a friend, who had no intention of seeing Marxzib in trouble.

"How on Zumt did this happen, my man? This is bad, really bad." He caught up with Marxzib, all huffing and puffing.

"Come on, Zebero. You know what we do. This is our job. We may have gone too far this time, but things happen in the field. Situations evolve. It isn't the theft - it's the getting caught that damages the most." Marxzib sounded rational in the comfort of his friend.

"Thank you for the wisdom, buddy," Zebero said with an oblique smile, "Have you planned how you will un-do this?"

"Well, I hope Kubo has saved some of her vehicle. We will know soon enough." Marxzib hit his sanbahak and disappeared. That is how people went from place to place in the seventh millennium.

18

Kubo's Story

Planet Ulna, Northern Milky-Way.

Kubo zipped through space to reach Ilna, a lush terrestrial planet home to her foster father. Ilna was one of the significant discoveries during the late space age of yore. Settlers had flocked to the planet for better prospects. It offered ample food, clean air, and drinkable water. Ilna had become a bustling and hustling place within the northern galaxy. Kubo grew up on Ilna after the death of her parents in a cosmic event. Wajko Pulo raised her much like his own daughter. Wajko was a sweet person, the kindest Kubo had seen. She called him Pop-Pop.

Wajko liked to work with his hands; he detested machines. He was busy crafting a statue from rare wood, and as usual, Kubo startled him with a hop.

"Goodness gracious me. You will kill your old man one of these days, Kubo," Wajko said as he tried to settle his hammering heart.

"Common Pop-Pop, I know you like it." Kubo hugged him tight and tugged at his long beard.

Wajko was delighted to see her. He patted her head. "When are you going to grow up, my child? I worry about you all the time."

Kubo looked at him with puppy eyes. "Pop-pop. I am twenty-one now! Don't worry about me. I can handle myself. You know I work for the conglomerate. I get to hobnob with influential people."

"That is what worries me, child. You cannot trust politicians. Can't you do something else?"

"What else would I do Pop-Pop? I am doing what I love the most, and I am good at it. That's all that matters."

Wajko's chest heaved with a heavy breath as worries clouded his mind. He could not change how he was wired. He was to all that met him, the most kind-hearted fellow one could come across, and his heart was centered on Kubo.

"What happened to all the statues you had done Pop-Pop," Kubo pointed to an empty rack as she popped a can of soda.

"I donated those statuettes. Some kids wanted them for school projects."

"You can't just give away stuff Pop-Pop. Everyone who asks does not always have good intentions. And what kids? I won't be surprised if those statuettes turn up on the black market for a cheap sale."

"Do you think so Kubo? Let's go and check with uncle Oip. He has a sharp nose for such things," Wajko said. "And be that as it may, child, one should never say no. Who knows when God could come to you asking something."

"Oh, my god! Pop-Pop," Kubo groaned in disbelief. "That legend is from some Earthen Age Tolstoy story. God doesn't do that anymore to anyone Pop-Pop. These are different times."

"Hmm. Not much has changed from the time when Tolstoy lived among humans, has it? I mean, apart from the Cosmic deaths. We are still the same people. We laugh, cry, and hate each other. Cheat, thieve, smile."

"I guess you are right, Pop-Pop," Kubo said, "But the world isn't as straightforward as you think it is. People can be mean."

And then she became silent. Her eyes changed their hues from a bright sunny morning to a dark, brooding afternoon.

"What's on your mind, Kubo? I can see something raging through that little head of yours. Out with it now."

"It's nothing Pop-Pop. It's just that," Kubo hesitated.

"I know what bothers you. It is natural for you to learn more about your people. Please do not think that I am offended."

"But wait, how did you…?"

"Know? Well, I am your Pop-Pop, aren't I?" Wajko smiled.

"Tell me something more, Pop-Pop. I want to go and see the home my folks lived in. This has been bothering me for a long time. It's all I think about when I close my eyes. I need some closure."

"Let us do something about it, then. All I was told from the child protection council was that your parents lived in the Sixnip galaxy. Now that is quite a ways from here. I do not know what nation they belonged to," Wajko said in an affectionate, comforting tone.

"Do you know anyone who could help? Finding their home in the giant Sixnips will be like searching for a needle in a haystack, Pop-Pop."

"Who else would know more than Oip, that crazy old fox?"

"Good old uncle Oip, hoorah!" Kubo jumped in glee, "Let's go and see him today!"

19

The Psychic

The Artisan's Colony on Planet Ilna, Northern Milky Way.

Oip looked the part. He wore black robes made from pure silk, ordered from a small colony on the earthen moon. Some artisans had chosen to live closer to the Earth and carry the baton of finer things. The little colony had soon become a space pit for tourists visiting Earth.

"Ho- ho- ho." Oip got up from his majestic wooden chair as he saw Kubo and Wajko appear from the mist.

"Look who we have here today. Kubo, my beloved child!"

Kubo jumped at him. "Uncle Oip! You look the same. Looks like some magic potion of yours is keeping you from growing old."

"Come on Kubo. He looks way old for his age. I look younger!" Wajko said in mock annoyance.

"Ignore him, shall we, Kubo? The old horse is just jealous of me, isn't he?"

Everyone laughed. Oip took them to his chambers and showed his latest collection of indigenous artifacts, some old fossils recovered from planet Earth. Racks and racks full of voodoo and magic stuff.

Oip also ordered some Palpanese food for them. He was pleased to see old Wajko and Kubo. He and Wajko were friends of more than fifty years. They had grown up together and lived on the same planet for almost all their lives. Both of them had no other family.

"In a way, we are like Immanuel Kant, a great philosopher from the Earthen Age. It is said he never left his hometown." Oip used to boast to Wajko when they were alone, chatting over cold glasses of sheer.

Wajko used to laugh him off. "Kant moved mountains. What have we achieved, my friend? We are the regular ones. The common Joes."

"Are you suggesting our lives carry no significance, Wajko?" Oip would question.

"No, they do." Wajko would respond, "We contribute to the universe by being in it. We help it run."

Oip and Wajko belonged to a generation that needed little to do with the entirety of the universe. For them, life was what they wanted it to be.

"I shall die regretless in this tiny abode of mine, Wajko," Oip would quip at times when they got serious about things. "I carried no inheritance, and I shall leave none behind. I have pledged all my art to the Metro Galactic Museum of human arts."

"You are a noble person, my friend," Wajko would say, his eyes reflecting his love and pride for his only friend. "We had nothing," Wajko would continue, "When we came to this world. And who knows what becomes of us when we die. I am not taking anything with me. I have seen too many people die in my long life. It's a lonely endeavor, death is. Billions and billions of people have lived and died before us. The wheel has kept on course."

"Well said, Wajko. Imagine the curiosity our ancestors from the Earthen Age had. They were not able to cross the moon's orbit for a very long time. Until a brilliant mind from a tiny village in Africa came up with the theory of attenuating space."

"Oh, that took so long, didn't it. I guess a few centuries matter much more to us than they do to this universal machine. As much as it is fascinating, it troubles me, Oip."

"Why would you trouble yourself with these, umm, morbid questions, my old pal." Wajko would say as they helped themselves to some more freshly brewed sheer.

As a child, Kubo would happily sit with these two, fidgeting her legs back and forth. They discussed more profound subjects but avoided morbid thoughts in front of the young child.

Preserving human art was important for Wajko. He did not want them to perish in the whirlwind of time. He did not believe human beings had changed since the onset of humanity on planet Earth. Cosmic death, too, existed for a long time. It was only that no one understood it back then.

"I have a question for you, uncle Oip. Two, really." Kubo said as she chomped on some Palpanese noodles.

"The first and most important one," she looked at Wajko, "Did those kids cheat Pop-Pop. He tells me he gave them a whole bunch of statues he had built with great labor."

Oip stopped munching. He was obviously amused to see good old Wajko being fooled. He saw this as an opportunity to tease him.

"Do you mean them Hij-kp kids - they sure as Zumt must have! Do you want me to look into it, Wajko?"

"You sure look happy, you dirty fox," Wajko scowled.

"Cool it, Pop-Pop. He is only trying to help us."

"Is he now? To me, it looks like he is looking for an excuse to deride me and bother me for the next six months, by telling me how naïve I am."

"I do not intend to do any such thing, Wajko," Oip said with a Miles-like tone.

"Oh, my god. You guys still watch that show, don't you? That stuff's like three millennia old!" Kubo referred to an ancient television show, full to the brim with maverick characters and their playful word-puns.

"Four, to be precise - and you have to accept the fact that it was a classic," Oip replied.

"For the most part, maybe," Kubo shrugged. "But see how they treated Jess. Not cool. Thanks to the feminists in the late twenty-first century, they stopped doing that on TV."

"They treated her well, didn't they?" Oip looked perplexed as he said this to Wajko.

"Well, you have to admit there were some parts. Like when anyone could kiss Jess if they had to pretend she was their girlfriend. I mean, I am not surprised women took an objection to that." Wajko replied.

Oip shook his head. "You know what? You are right, Kubo. Now you have spoiled it for me!"

"Anyways what was your second question?" Oip said.

"Well. Umm. I don't know how to say this. Help me here, Pop-Pop."

"She wants to visit her roots in the Sixnips, Oip," Wajko said, his voice shaking a little.

"The Sixnips! That is a long way from here. At least, that's what I have heard."

"That's what Pop-Pop tells me, uncle Oip," Kubo bit her lip. "Also, I don't know where they lived. I don't mind the distance, there are better medicines available now to deal with the space lag effect. I know some from my place of work, some cutting-edge stuff."

"Would you know any further, Oip? Or know anyone who does?" Wajko asked as he pushed a bowl of Jkio grass soup aside that had barely been touched. "I do not want to send her alone out there. It's a big bad universe. We need to know better. Find some friends if we may."

"I hear you." Oip said, "I will ask around; I know someone there, a fellow intellectual. She will certainly help."

"You would do that for me?" Kubo chirped. "Thank you, uncle Oip."

"You bet, my child."

Kubo tilted her head ever so slightly and smiled. She appeared relieved for the first time since she had arrived on Ilna. Both Wajko and Oip knew how much this mattered to her. And Oip genuinely wanted to help Kubo, more for the sake of Wajko. Both of them were ready to help her in any way they could.

That's how friends are, they help each other out.

20
MARXZIB'S DILEMMA
The ShoeBox, Capital District of CLAN.

MARXZIB DROOPED LOW IN his chair looking at the large screens before him. He had scoured through thousands of documents and ran scores of programs in an attempt to rebuild the vehicle that Kubo had built.

I should have never asked her to destroy the Zumting thing. He thought as he pumped bubbles into a large glass of soda, packed to the brim with ice, for the hundredth time that day.

"I can't find her boss," Uxa shouted from her cube. "I have tried every trick in the book. It's like she's vanished from the universe."

Marxzib pushed himself out of the comfortable chair and went over to her.

"What do you mean vanished? Surely, she must have left some trace, some contact?" Marxzib said as he leaned onto a large pillar nearby. There he stood with his legs crossed. A permanent look of displeasure was plastered on his face these days. He then turned toward Akan and said, "What do you think, Champ? You must know something about her, don't you people hang out together all the time?"

"Honestly, I thought I did know about her. But nothing has been helpful so far. I even tried her foster father on Ilna. Nothing." Akan stuck his neck out of his cubicle. He had his eternal look of confusion on.

"What did he say, her dad?"

"He says he hasn't heard from her for a couple of weeks."

"Ok. Here's the deal." Marxzib said, "We must find whether the horse she built actually touched any CERS systems. Can you guys investigate? Scour the perimeter again if needed."

Both Uxa and Akan looked perplexed.

"I'm sorry, boss? Are we to breach the perimeter again? Hasn't that landed us in big trouble already?" Uxa said, her eyes widened with surprise.

"I feel the same way, boss," Akan pitched in. "I think we should stay away from this as much as possible."

Marxzib was both surprised and annoyed at the team's pushback on this. But he remained calm. He knew he would have to trust the team to get the proof he needed.

"I understand your concern, guys, believe me, I do, but we need to do this. It's our job for Zumt's sake!"

"But" Uxa scratched her head, "I don't understand this. What exactly are we trying to do here?"

"Good question," Marxzib replied, "The idea here, is to prove that we never touched any of the CERS systems. Instead, Kubo found the Blueprint, lying un-protected on one of the random servers. It's been termed as an incursion, we want to spin-doctor it and prove that it was an accident, nothing more."

Marxzib tried explaining the rationale. But the team did not look convinced, he was met with worried faces.

"How will that help us, boss, or anyone for that matter?" Akan asked, not out of sarcasm but out of genuine curiosity.

"It's for the President, really," Marxzib said. "Like I explained earlier, she can take this evidence and basically explain that this was not a spying attempt - but an unintended security lapse. That might dampen the damage a bit, or at least give some time for the President to stall, a much-needed breather in this political storm."

"But this does involve sabotage, boss. First, we will need a complete copy of the Blueprint," Uxa said, "And second, a reverse timestamp that indicates the Blueprint was placed there, let's say, a month ago, much before we found it. That, in my mind, is rigging. We cannot possibly do this without altering the stamps."

"I agree with her," said Akan, "Any such attempt requires encroaching on the CERS territory one more time. What if we get caught?"

"Listen, guys, I understand the risks involved. But we need to do this anyway. It's important." Marxzib tried to reason with them.

Akan and Uxa looked at each other. *"It's important"* was not the explanation that would convince them. Uxa was shaking her head in disbelief. She thought for a minute or so and then said, "I am sorry, boss. I won't do this. I go to university later this year. I have already spent three years doing this thankless job, don't want to sabotage my chances by going all rogue like this."

"She is right, boss!" Akan said. His shoulders eased, and a tinge of confidence shone in his eyes. He was relieved Uxa took this stand. "I'm sorry, but I can't do this either. You can fire me for this, but this does not sound like a sane thing to do. It's outrageous!"

Marxzib looked at their faces one by one. *I taught them like my students- is this how they repay me? This is bullshit. This can't be happening.* He moved away from them and started pacing the room, rubbing his hands, muttering, and mumbling.

Akan and Uxa, being the young people they were, did not know how to react to the irrational behavior of their boss. They just looked at each other and made incomprehensible gestures.

A few minutes passed like this. Then Marxzib said, "You know what, you both can leave for now. I will call you if I need anything."

Akan and Uxa left the room without saying a single word. Marxzib wasn't sure what his options were at this juncture. On the one hand, he wanted to help Zxea in the crunch hour; on the other hand, his team had raised some very valid concerns. He sat staring at the sky from his window for a long time. Then texted Kamado on his Vabaka.

"It's Marxzib here. I am sorry, I don't see any way to control the damage for now. Please proceed with other options as you may see fit."

21
It's Business
Planet K000-9, Neutral Zone 1.

Kwaqa was confused.

"Didn't we sell this information to the CERS only recently?"

"Well, well!" Xules went into his Zen voice and said, "Information serves many purposes. For some, information is simply a deterrent; for others, it is a call to action. And for a select few like us, it's plain and simple leverage. We *must* use it to increase our importance in the galactic play."

"But the Syndicate is dangerous, isn't it?" She said with an air of anxiety.

"It is dangerous, it sure as Zumt is. But then, our job is complicated by design. We take risks every day. Some work while others don't. That doesn't stop us from doing what we do."

"And what happens when the Syndicate knows they've been sold information that already existed within the interested party? Won't that put us in jeopardy?"

"It may very well do that, but you see, Kwaqa - the Syndicate is not going to reach out to the CERS. Instead, they will try to strong-arm President Zxea and extract their pound of flesh. That I know for sure."

"But why wouldn't they go to the CERS?"

"Chief Ukama hates the Syndicate."

"Really? I thought the Syndicate was the commander in chief's hidden political ally" Kwaqa said.

"Well, you did not let me finish my sentence there, Kwaqa. What I was going to say is that the chief hates the Syndicate these days. The region's politics have taken a turn. Chief Ukama is trying hard to remain popular and relevant. There has been much hate mongering in the region; many blame Ukama for promoting it indirectly. If he wants to get elected again the conservative vote alone will not be enough. So, to mollycoddle the liberals, he has had to crack down on illegal activities of the Syndicate. This has strained the weird bonhomie between the hawkish chief and the Syndicate."

"Humm. I wish I could understand the nitty-gritty like you someday," Kwaqa said with a slight bit of admiration for her boss.

"You will get there, Kwaqa. You are a quick study. You need to keep your eyes open and, um, read some of those opinion pieces and the editorials in the policy newspapers."

"Newspapers? Do they still exist?" Kwaqa said with a pronounced roll of her eyes.

"Yes, they do, and so do the conglomerate gazettes. Though only a few people read them. Some very useful information lives there. For instance, I recently learned that a business controlled by the chief's family has landed him in soup. Apparently, Chief Ukama's son-in-law owns a significant stake in a firm called Thexacorp. This firm has drilling interests on abandoned planets and X-Lands. Now even in a conservative party like Ukama's Torial, there are some who worry about environmental damage. There is talk of corruption and kickbacks involved as well. That cannot be ignored."

"Looks like the son-in-law is making hay. So long as he keeps the Chief's daughter happy," Kwaqa quipped.

They both laughed.

"But boss, common logic would suggest we are double-crossing people here and creating powerful enemies for ourselves in return. What if the Syndicate knows we have already approached the CERS?" Kwaqa continued with her previous worries.

"Politics and poetry betray logic, Kwaqa." Xules was consistently patient in his analyses. "We must be able to read the fine print and make the most for ourselves. We may be overplaying our hands at certain times, but that is bound to happen. Nothing should stop us from achieving our goals."

22
Ghirnot Plans for the Future
Undisclosed destination.

Ghirnot was playing the ancient game of chess on a large chess board made of vintage silk cloth, crowded with marble pieces. Like several other things, the advent of artificial intelligence had irradicated the game of chess. It was now known only to a handful of curious aficionados.

"Permission to speak, Senator." Chaliza said as he walked in.

Ghirnot looked up at him. "Of course, Chaliza. And you do not need to address me as senator anymore. Let us be practical here."

Chaliza half smiled. As a loyal employee of several years, he knew Ghirnot was unpredictable. "I understand that sir, but I call you that out of respect."

"Ask what you want to."

"I want to know about your plans, Sir. We have been hiding out here for a while now. I am getting bored with it."

"Bored?" Ghirnot made a face. "That is not an option for strategists and power players like us. We must be thinking and strategizing all the time."

"Strategize for what?" Chaliza shrugged. "It's time we realize your career, and mine along with it, of course - is over, sir."

Ghirnot got up from his seat and looked at Chaliza.

"Are you out of your mind, Chaliza?"

"I am sorry, Sir, but look around us. What do you see? We are hiding like fugitives. As a matter of fact, we *are* fugitives."

"So?"

"I do not see any honorable road leading us back to the Capital District. They have barred you for life from contesting any elections. I am implicated as your co-conspirator in so many things I have lost count. No matter who comes to rule the house, no one will welcome you back in the fold - unless some miracle happens."

Ghirnot let out a huge and scary laugh. He spread his arms, looked up, and roared, "This here, me, standing in front of you, Chaliza - is the miracle."

Chaliza could not believe his eyes. *He is losing it. No, he has lost it completely. Zumting Ghirnot has finally lost his Zumting mind. A fugitive riddled with delusions of grandeur. Delusional idiot!*

He took a minute to gather his thoughts and said, "I beg your pardon, Sir. I don't get what you are saying. I simply don't."

"What part of this do you not understand, Chaliza?"

Chaliza did not respond.

"That was a rhetorical question, Chaliza. I will tell you why. You are looking at it from the wrong angle. You were right when you said there is no road for us leading to the Capital District. I would improve that sentence slightly - by adding the word *democratic* before the road."

Chaliza shrunk his shoulders into his neck and said, "Ok, I get that, sir. But how do we take over a mighty state like the CLAN?"

"If you look at human history, you will find several examples."

"Of?"

"Of how mighty people snatch power back, even after losing everything they once had."

"I still do not understand."

"Ok. Here's an example. Back in the fifth millennium, the state of Irschia had banished General Fiho to exile for plotting a coup. Everyone thought that was it for the general. But this general was a resilient fella. He crossed over into the neighboring planet state of Klia, forged an alliance with their military, and attacked his now estranged home state of Irschia. Klian forces eventually subdued Irschia and made Fiho the new ruler. He ruled there single handedly for almost thirty years."

"Ok, so let us say you are General Fiho," Chaliza said.

"Now you are thinking." Ghirnot smiled.

"But who is Klia?"

"Think some more - who benefits the most if the Milky Way is thrown into disarray?"

"The Magnonians?"

"Dead right. The Alpha Magnon. That, my friend, is our highway back to the Capital District."

23
The Syndicate
Planet K000-9, Neutral Zone 1.

"Xules, trust means nothing to us. It's a phony construct. We do not deal in such currency." Ohuima spoke with utmost clarity.

"Anyways, why do you even care about trust?" Pwesdra said, her lip curled with disdain.

Xules smiled. "Irrespective of my reputation, as you ladies would appreciate - I am an absolute gentleman. In that sense, I want to gain your trust by giving you highly classified information that you can profit from. My trusted informers tell me the Syndicate has been – well, how do I put this – struggling with making profits lately."

"Be that as it may," Pwesdra peered down at Xules, "Conventional wisdom tells me I should not believe you. After all, you have quite the reputation of being a notorious conman, my dear Xules."

"Why, I assume we are fairly similar in that vein. If the market wisdom out there has to be believed, the Syndicate has managed to somehow lose the trust of most of the key players in the market. I may have suffered a few minor setbacks, which you so unkindly referred to as the results of my conmanship, on *conmanry* rather. Wonder which fits the best." Xules was blabbering now.

"Focus, boss." Kwaqa whispered in his ears. "This isn't the time to be witty. Don't bore them to death!"

"I like what you did there, Kwaqa." Xules said in a voice that was audible to the Syndicate reps. "I am sorry, ladies. My young colleague here and I cannot help but make puns whenever an opportunity presents itself. One must always be in their element, shouldn't they, no matter what the situation."

"Well, I can tell you about this *situation* for one." Pwesdra said, Xules could see her face all tensed up. "Your jokes are quintessential duds. And you are wasting our time. If you don't get on with it in the next few minutes, your opportunity is a goner."

"Well, here's the thing," Xules started hurriedly, only partially realizing the extent of the damage he had been inflicting on his audience's ears with his watered-down puns.

"I am sure you must be aware of the military tensions between the CLAN and the CERS, the two nefarious Milky Way bullies, as I like to call them privately. While there hasn't been a major conflict as of yet, we have witnessed several smaller skirmishes over the past few decades. Now, the reason there hasn't been a full-scale war lies in the composition of the governments presiding over these bodies. It's liberals on both sides of the aisle. And liberals, as you know, are bad for business."

"You are wrong, Xules," Pwesdra again blocked him sternly. "The Torials are far from being liberals, and Chief Ukama is a hard ass, as hard as they come. He and that little assistant of his are hell-bent on establishing their supremacy." Pwesdra was obviously talking about Kimnabav here.

"As a fellow woman," Kwaqa jumped right in and blurted out, "You should avoid using adjectives such as little, pretty, etc., for women, Kvazim. This is the seventh millennium, for Zumt's sake."

Pwesdra straightened, her nostrils flared at Kwaqa's interruption, as she answered tersely, "Point taken, but your boss here is obviously wrong and has been wasting our time."

"You are correct in saying Chief Ukama is a hardliner," Xules continued, fully ignoring the criticism, his face incredibly passive. "However, the liberals within his party manage to thwart him most of the time. Dulerty, one of his most powerful generals, is a softy."

"We are running in loops here, overstating the obvious. What is your case, Xules?" Ohuima intervened, seeing as the conversation was not going anywhere.

"I am coming to that, Kvazim," Xules replied hastily. "Recently, there has been an illegal incursion from some of President Zxea's team - right into the nucleus of the CERS."

"That's just baloney. The CERS's defense is airtight. There is no way anyone's even going near the T13." Pwesdra did not know how to mince words.

A broad grin came over Xules's face. The Syndicate rep was talking in his language now. "But that is precisely what they have managed to do, Kvazim Pwesdra. A highly covert team working exclusively for the President was able to breach the perimeter and rebuild the CERS's Blueprint by combining thousands of scattered data artifacts."

Ohuima snorted. "Ok, speaking theoretically, let us say this is possible. But do you have any proof of this? Encroaching the CERS's limits would be a dreadful offense. These types of things could easily trigger wars."

"Yes!" said Xules emphatically, "I have obtained infallible proof from one of the people who worked on this mission. President Zxea has this henchman, Marxzib, who does her dirty laundry for her. This was all his making."

"So, what do you want from us? We are not a player in this, are we?" Pwesdra leaned forward toward Xules, looking mildly interested.

"Yeah, what's in it for you, Xules? And more importantly- for us," Ohuima raised her eyebrows. "Looks like you have some agenda in this. Are you trying to settle some old scores here – over our shoulders?"

"Yeah, I also saw the scorn on your face when you mentioned Marxzib. Is he an old enemy of yours? I always have doubts when it comes to you, Xules."

Pwesdra hated Xules and made no effort to conceal it. Xules tried to be cordial with her regardless, laboring to keep a good working relationship going. The Syndicate was a large galactic entity. Smaller operatives like Xules depended on it for bigger jobs. And this job, in his eyes, was the motherlode.

Kwaqa was not happy with this idea of Xules. She was anxious about dealing with the Syndicate; she knew how dangerous these people were. She had raised her concerns with Xules, but he was convinced this was the right thing to do. So, they decided to approach Pwesdra and Ohuima. Pwesdra looked after the Syndicate's heavy metals dealings in the X-Lands region, while Ohuima was the kingpin for all political wheeling and dealing. Pwesdra was an angry woman known for her bluntness. Ohuima was the quiet one. But between the two, they had the most lucrative of the Syndicate's business handled.

Xules knew Ohuima from his younger days. One of his friends, Ribej, used to date her. Eventually, Ribej and Ohuima broke up, but Ohuima and Xules remained in touch.

"Ohuima, you've known me for, what, twenty years now? You must go with me on this." Xules tried to evoke loyalty from their friendship. His credo was to do whatever it took.

"You know I do not mix friendship and business, Xules," Ohuima responded quietly. "Besides, for us to take this to the bosses, there are two conditions. One, this information should lead us directly to some material gain. And second, it must be authenticated by a third party. I cannot trust your intel blindly. That's not how we roll."

Pwesdra frowned. She was not happy with Ohuima's apparent interest in Xules's proposal. She wanted to brush off Xules completely. But Ohuima was her partner, and she trusted her judgment.

"That is a fair expectation. I will transfer the data to your Vabaka right away. You can get it verified from your trusted resources. As to how this can be used, I have some schemes in mind. Which I shall discuss with you and your bosses once they are on board with this idea."

"Oh really?" Pwesdra furrowed her eyebrows, "Do you think we are THAT stupid? We need to know everything to the last detail if you want anything from us. Else we are out of here."

Ohuima was startled at the sudden outrage from Pwesdra, but she also felt Xules was being a little condescending in his latest remark.

Pwesdra shot an angry look at Xules. Then she turned to Ohuima and said, "I will be honest with you. I don't trust this fella. I feel like there is more to this than he is letting on. And if you remember, he had us almost killed on Zumt."

"Well, that was only a misunderstanding, Kvazim Pwesdra, and I knew the commandos were coming to rescue you!" Xules tried to intervene hurriedly.

"*Uh oh, this is trouble,*" Kwaqa thought. She had heard the story several times; her boss had basically messed up and taken off, leaving Pwesdra and Ohuima behind in enemy territory.

"Stop bullshitting Xules. You put us in harm's way and then took off like a coward. I call it a betrayal. I don't know what you consider it, Ohuima," Pwesdra fumed.

"Take it easy, Pwesdra. It was a tough situation for all of us. And I don't believe in holding grudges forever. If this intel can help the Syndicate, we must take it ahead. We are required by our job to do so," Ohuima got up from her seat and shot back at Xules. "I am taking a gamble with you in this, champ. But I would strongly advise not offending the people you want favors from."

Xules laughed sheepishly and for too long. Kwaqa let out an annoyed huff.

24
THE RIOK TAKES CHARGE
The People's Nation of Priscia, Neutral Zone 4.

PRISCIAN INTELLIGENCE BROUGHT NEWS. The CERS was considering launching a full-scale war on the CLAN in light of the recent hacking scandal. It was said that the president of the CLAN had ordered an unprovoked breach into the CERS's safety systems, and the hawks within the CERS administration were more than willing to consider this an act of war.

"An enemy vehicle entered our territory unprovoked. We consider this an attack on our sovereignty." A senior CERS politician was heard saying.

Priscia was the meditation hub for the Milky Way. People flocked to boot camps in theology and metaphysical sciences from all over. Lroki Oima, a Priscian professor, was a celebrity thinker with followers from across the universe. His opponents criticized him for monetizing traditional meditative practices. But Priscia was a free-thinking nation, and everyone was allowed to do what they felt was good for them. Priscians were abreast with the latest technological advances, but they had not let go of their meditative core. They traded freely with both the south and the north and welcomed anyone who wanted to live in Priscia with open arms.

Kinmuk Wey, the current Riok, believed this could become the way of the universe. The Priscian values of peace and non-alignment could make the Milky Way become one, and people could move freely without restrictions.

Like Kinmuk was subjected to now, Pihimay Wey and her fellow founders had considered what would happen if a full-fledged intra-galactic conflict scenario occurred. Only it was at the time when the constitution of Priscia was being drafted.

"The people's nation of Priscia shall abstain from hostility toward other entities within the Milky Way galaxy and beyond. In the event of a full-blown intergalactic conflict, whether caused by political reasons or otherwise, the people of Priscia shall maintain their neutral stance and resist any internal temptations to align with the northern or the southern conglomerates. This is the will of the elders of Priscia that shall be respected by the generations to come. The people believe in peace for humankind to survive unharmed for millennia."

***

"Do I have permission to speak?" Aeqima bowed to the Riok.

"Of course, Aeqima. You do not have to ask me for permission. I greatly respect your knowledge."

"Thank you, master. You are the chosen leader of the People of Priscia. We must express our gratitude and respect."

"Please go on, Aeqima; what do you make of this whole situation?"

"The constitution asks us to refrain, my master." Aeqima said politely. "The founders had explicitly mentioned a full-fledged war."

"I wonder why they would mention it. I get that there always was a possibility. But in these times, large-scale wars are not common."

"I believe some future simulation might have been at the play master. There was a great Priscia statistician by the name of Wqiya Jaken. She had built some models that have withstood centuries."

Kinmuk took a long breath and got up from the floor where he was perched, meditating. He slowly walked over to the wall that had photographs of the previous Rioks arranged in rows. He looked at them almost aimlessly for a while. Aeqima stood in the room, observing him silently. She knew the Riok had a habit of slipping into spells of contemplation during conversations.

"I wish the conglomerates did not act with such impulse. I used to believe that President Zxea was the level-headed one. She would never allow warmongers to have their way. And the CERS too. Chief Ukama came across as a balanced politician to me."

Aeqima seemed to agree as she'd nodded while he spoke, "If we are to believe, my master, a careless act of aggression from the CERS has pushed the wall."

"I am certain there is more to the story than meets the eye. There must be some aspect that everyone has overlooked. There is this endless *Śūnyatā* around us, a nothingness. We all try to find meaning for ourselves in it. Things are not what they appear to be. It is our perceptions of things that lead us to form opinions."

Kinmuk wanted to believe in Zxea. But their tradition was to stay impartial. Stay non-aligned.

Kinmuk crossed the room toward a massive glass window. He stood there quietly, observing the vast expanse leading up to the great Priscian Mountain ranges. Mount Uho stood tall in the distance. Its peak was covered in snow even in the warmer months.

"There stands mount Uho. With all our pride and our devotions. We must hold our heads high and take a stance."

"What are you thinking, master?" Aeqima asked.

"We all seek balance of perspectives, to maintain our sanity as thinking beings. This magnificent galaxy, too, needs a balance."

"A balance of power?" Aeqima asked.

"Yes. A balance of power, resources, and rights. Powerful elements from conglomerates have for long plundered ore from planets. Abused the galaxy's resources for their greed. They played their games, and we watched in silence."

Aeqima nodded. "Master, the case of Planet BVIOP 1 stands out as evidence."

"Remind me, please, if you do not mind, Aeqima. I have forgotten the minutiae."

"I am happy to, master." Aeqima said as she started narrating the story. "It was some time ago; the planet was a bustling market space. People all over the Milky Way flocked to the planet to buy and sell goods. Incidentally, there was a middleman, a small-time hustler named Xules, who scoured the galaxy to find cheap buys. Once he arrived on the planet, he discovered that the local merchants were selling a type of stone named Glycera at throwaway prices. Being of a sharp business mind, Xules was intrigued and wanted to explore further. After doing some research, he learned that the oar could be used to manufacture microchips for Vabakas, the most common type of communication device used these days. A fact the local merchants were utterly unaware of."

"Ah. Isn't that typical?" The Riok said, "It always takes an outsider, for better or for worse."

"Yes, master!" Clearly, Aeqima was having fun narrating the story. "With this information in hand, Xules procured substantial amounts of the stone and sold it at a premium in other marketplaces. It is rumored that he reaped significant profits from the trade. However, the local residents soon took notice and began to follow him, realizing they were undervaluing the rock. The news quickly spread, triggering a frenzied rush for Glycera that was reminiscent of the California gold rush on Earth many millennia ago."

"The avarice of humankind. No wonder our ancestors prohibited all forms of mining." The Riok contemplated.

"Politicians from both sides," Aeqima continued, "In cahoots with large corporations, quickly grasped the significance of the planet and the abundance of Glycera that could be found with minimal effort. The locals, driven by the profits from selling the ore, also began to capitalize on the opportunity. The price of the ore skyrocketed as bidding wars erupted, and in the race to mine the stone, people began raising their homes. In a matter of weeks, mining companies, led by a firm called Thexacorp, popped up all over the place, and in less than a year, the planet was completely stripped of its resources, rendering it nearly uninhabitable. What happened to the planet stands as a prime example of a capitalism-driven doomsday scenario."

"I wonder what became of the people of the planet." The Riok looked away from the window. His eyes looked dull by weariness.

"Some made a profit and flew to other planets to live opulent lives with the money. Others were not so lucky. They had to be evacuated and lifted to other planets as part of President Zxea's humanitarian mission."

"A benevolent cause indeed. How could President Zxea get drawn into this power struggle? She is a kind soul."

"Well, in the case of BVIOP, it seems she was tormented by guilt. It was a moral dilemma for her. Even though traders from both sides were involved, it was clear that the CLAN businesses benefited the most from the exploitation. President Zxea felt a sense of responsibility and took swift action. Perhaps she faces the same now."

"Wasn't she nominated for the Jeeble prize that year? They rejected the nomination, though, those Jeeble snobs."

Aeqima smiled at this. "Yes, she probably does not fit their bill, master."

"Nor would I," he said, quickly realizing he was boasting. "Not to say I would ever be nominated or have any such aspirations!"

"Master, you would be the ideal candidate for the Jeeble prize. Aeqima paused to look up at the mountains past the Riok's shoulder before lowering her gaze back down to him, "The current crisis presents a great opportunity for us to establish ourselves as the third power."

"Indeed, Aeqima. The time has come to disrupt the galactic order of power. We must set the third front in motion. Re-establish the balance." Kinmuk replied, "I will dictate a letter addressed to all galactic nations now. Please begin reaching out to planetary authorities."

Aeqima was delighted with the Riok's response. She had pushed the previous Rioks to be more engaged in galactic politics, but their meditative natures prevented them from pursuing power. This was a rare opportunity, and Aeqima was prepared to seize it.

25

Kubo's Journey

Planet Ilna, Northern Milky Way.

At twenty-one, Kubo was more mature than other people her age. She often wondered why a cosmic event should pick her parents, such vivacious young people in their mid-thirties, full of life. She had lost her childhood to the overwhelming grief of waking up in a world that did not have a loving father and a doting mother. Ugoz, her boyfriend, was her anchor through all her emotional turmoil. She wanted to see him once before embarking on the voyage.

***

They met at their usual place, a park bench on a small hill among trees. Kubo's planned trip to the Sixnips weighed heavily on both of their minds.

"Do you have to go there? Can I persuade you not to, Kubo?"

"I need to do this, Ugoz. I desperately need this closure."

"Do you want to talk about it?" Ugoz said in a voice filled with love and care.

"I don't know how to describe it, Ugoz. Abstract, blurry thoughts. Flashes of people and things. Places too. And they do not come to me when I am focusing on them. These things hit me out of the blue, leaving me in turmoil."

"But how? I do not understand."

"For instance, this one day, I was in the middle of a meeting with my colleagues. And suddenly a landscape flashed in front of my eyes. A beautiful garden, ledges of bright flowers. And there, I saw my parents. They were just sitting on the grass, probably looking at the setting sun. The sky was a beautiful crimson red. My mom's head rested on my dad's shoulders. They both looked so much at peace. Everything they longed for existed at that moment. The sunset, the evening, the flowers and-"

"And what, Kubo?" Ugoz moved closer to Kubo and put his arms around her. She leaned back against him.

"And the love, Ugoz. Like they had found this all-illusive emotion - the feeling of love. I could see it in their eyes. And it made me feel I was there with them in that surreal moment. Looking out into the expansive green pastures. I was living and breathing with them, a thinking entity. A heart beating in tandem with their hearts."

"Maybe they had conceived you back then, Kubo. That might explain your memories. It is strange how memories work. Memories from the mother's womb must hold some sway on our behavior."

"It hits me hard, Ugoz, that I have lost them forever. That I am not going to see them again in this life. This feeling ravages my body like a raging sword. I feel I am being shattered to shreds. Why did they have to leave so soon?"

"Hey, Kubo." Ugoz tried to console her. He leaned over and kissed her on her cheek gently. "Your parents loved you. A parent's love for their child is unconditional. Wherever they are, they must want you to stay happy."

Tears rolled from her eyes, and she started sobbing softly.

Part 2: A Storm Gathers

A month before the kill shot.

26

Tumults of War

CERS Headquarters, Southern Milky Way.

The CERS had assembled their top brass at Camp Erba, a quaint ranch on the well-designed planet of Fiopa. Every important player in the conglomerate was summoned, including representatives from security, intelligence, strategy, communications, fleet commanders, and captains. The beauty of Fiopa left no one unimpressed, making it the perfect setting for this gathering.

General Nodfi and Colonel Lopki were forbidden from attending the meeting, despite the vital information they had procured regarding the incursion. Chief Ukama was not happy with the way they had dealt with Xules. The chief believed Xules should have been dealt with a hammer hand and not a reward.

"There is no time for pleasantries." Chief Ukama started the proceedings right away. "The CLAN has committed an im-pardonable act of aggression that cannot be overlooked by us as a sovereign conglomerate. Our offense strategies have been created to safeguard us against precisely such deliberate assaults. We must rise to the challenge and prepare for an all-out war against the CLAN. It's time to teach them a lesson."

"Umm... Commander in Chief," a tentative voice emerged from the audience. It was Dulerty, head of the aviation and planetary security council. Dulerty was responsible for keeping the fleet ready and responsive at all times. The hesitation in his voice could be attributed to the rumors about the fact that there wasn't enough evidence of the breach or enough explanation on how the breach had damaged or posed a threat to the security of the CERS.

Dulerty stood up and cleared his throat. "May I say something?"

Ukama went ramrod straight, his focus moving to Dulerty. He wanted to get on with it; besides, he and Dulerty did not agree on a whole lot of issues. The chief felt Dulerty lacked the courage and aggression required to head the council.

"Now is the time to raise any objections, so please speak up, Commander."

"Thank you, honorable Chief," Dulerty said and then started to speak in a controlled but very polished manner, "My advisors and I do not feel we have sufficient proof to justify a full-scale war. The consequences of such a war could be catastrophic for the galaxy - it could last for years or even decades, and it's impossible to predict who would emerge victorious in such a massive undertaking. We need to send our inspectors to the CLAN and investigate if this was truly an error committed by their intelligence unit, as their president claims."

At least half of the crowd appeared to agree with the speaker, but several shook their heads in quiet disapproval, which did not go unnoticed.

It was evident that the congregation was divided, at least in the initial reactions. Senator Kimnabav, Chief Ukama's political advisor, raised her hand and requested to speak. Ukama acknowledged this welcome distraction. Kimnabav was a headstrong leader within the CERS, well-liked by many senior leaders, including the commander in chief. The CERS was currently run by an ultra-conservative delegation. Kimnabav's rhetoric mostly aligned with the delegation's agenda. The liberals, known as the leftists, back in the Earthen Age, did not appreciate her aggression. They feared that if she rose to power in the CERS, she might alter the policies and principles laid down by the constitution. The conservatives were not outright pro-war. In fact, half of them clearly opposed it. However, in a highly polarized universe, multiple misleading stereotypes were formed. Many Torials, such as General Dulerty, saw conservatism as a way of adhering to the well-defined social norms that allowed for society's better functions. Their version of conservatism had no place for hatred and warmongering. The Cabal was a different case in itself. It was an unabashedly pro-war clique with some outrageous, yet stubborn notions of the past. Kimnabav was practically born and raised in the Cabal and wholeheartedly carried forward their agenda.

The founders of the CERS had no intention of giving birth to an aggressive political force; they had believed in building a harmonious, unified conglomerate of planets, stars, and X-Lands that would provide a foundation for the betterment of the Milky Way galaxy.

"Our respected aviation and security council chief makes a serious argument. However, we have been neglecting similar acts of provocation from the CLAN for too long now; I, and several of my esteemed friends and colleagues, strongly believe that this is the time to teach a lesson to our enemies, once and for all." Kimnabav spoke with a confidence that bordered on arrogance.

"Aye, aye!" Many voices erupted from the supporters of the incumbent conglomerate.

"Unbelievable," Dulerty mumbled as he looked away. He believed that Kimnabav and other younger leaders under Ukama's tutelage were overly aggressive. Rikey, seated near Dulerty, could detect his annoyance. This brought to her mind something Dulerty had previously said about Kimnabav.

"She's worse than Ukama. I read a memo written by her; she wants to establish a supremacy of people that have come from the advanced regions of erstwhile planets. Her mother was a liberal icon, for Zumt's sake. What a travesty!"

Dulerty had asked his closest colleagues earlier to *"Stay cautious of a systemic initiative to throw the progressive CERS into primitive ways of hatred."*

As a close confidant of Dulerty's, Rikey was responsible for keeping a tab on hate mongers. She had maintained a fastidious log of hate comments on various social streams. While most of it was misinformation, there was no dearth of motivated propaganda aimed at creating rifts in the otherwise peace-loving and secular CERS.

Some of the comments were particularly hateful. One read, "Our forefathers established the CERS. The rest must follow our way of life. If they can't, they should go and live somewhere else. There is no dearth of terrestrial planets in the galaxy."

Another one read, "Look at these people. They eat meat. How could they? Don't they have any compassion left?"

Hatred was scattered equally on both sides. Meat eaters hated vegetarians. One said, "Isn't vegetarian food supposed to make you docile and peaceful? Look at how hostile these people are!"

There were some voices in the intelligentsia too. A learned hawk said, "We must, if we have to, go back to the border and immigration systems like those that existed in the Earthen Age. If you look at history closely, it is not difficult to understand that all men and women are not born equally."

Such talk scared Rikey. People like her and Dulerty were fast becoming outdated within the CERS administration. She was secretly worried Dulerty might not be allowed to complete his term and retire on his own terms.

But Dulerty was an old warrior; he wouldn't give up this easily.

"Comrades," he started to speak again as the voices clamoring in support of war began calming down. "I understand there is a desire to retaliate, which I would say is not unnatural given these circumstances. But as a galactic superpower, our responsibilities exceed our personal ambitions and desires. An emphatic win over the neighboring conglomerate is one such ambition we must not succumb to."

"I find your words offensive and hostile toward us," Kimnabav was quick to interject. "How could you question our patriotism, honorable Commander." She said firmly, "In calling this very natural response a personal ambition, you have made this issue political. I condemn your statements today and urge the council to support the commander in chief's decision on this issue."

Senator Jity, a close confidant of the chief and a silent observer thus far, did not like Kimnabav's attempt of seeking the council's approval before consulting with the chief. "Honorable colleague," Jity addressed Kimnabav, "I urge you to not jump ahead before the commander in chief completes his argument."

Jity was not comfortable with Kimnabav's rapid rise within the ranks *"How could she!"* he said to himself.

The chief looked at Kimnabav first and then Jity. This was his way of asking them to shut up.

The chief then said, "I can see that some of us are not convinced, but I want to assure all of you, respected representatives from planets and stars, X-Lands, and the asteroid colonies,"

"You seem to forget us, chief Ukama." Someone shouted in an angry voice from the assembly, interrupting Chief Ukama. It was Qwsxert, the representative from Fi-Lands.

"My apologies, Qwsxert, how could I forget you? It was a minor slip of mine that you should ignore with the big heart of yours." The chief tried to control the damage hurriedly.

Qwsxert gave an awkward laugh. Only to infuriate his people back home.

"And what about us, huh?" Shouted Azzkuyia, the representative from Qanet 221#.

"My apologies to you as well, Azzkuyia." The chief made an apparent show of regret, but he was fuming with rage within. To him, these people were suckers. They expected him to know the minutiae their life despite the fact that they chose to live in the most inaccessible locations.

Ukama, however, wasn't the only one frustrated with this. Many in the CERS were annoyed with the ultra-liberals who opted to establish colonies on long-distance asteroids, X-Lands, Fi-Lands, and Qanets too.

"Let us put this to vote, honorable Commander in Chief." A calm voice emerged. It was Fimlop. She was the head of the conglomerate affairs council. In the assembly, her decisions were a mandate to everyone, including the chief. "Since there is a clear division among members of this esteemed council, I recommend we conduct a poll to seek a clear mandate."

Ukama was not happy. His face turned stiff. He wanted to protest, but his political sense advised him otherwise. He chose to stay calm and nodded his head in agreement.

Fimlop could sense his anger, but she didn't care for personal feelings. Her job demanded she remain neutral. "Let us all meet back early next week, after which there shall be a vote as to the response of the conglomerate and her people."

Ukama doubted the legitimacy of democratic approaches to war. Even if Fimlop were to defeat him using parliamentary tactics, he was prepared to sabotage his own troops to build a façade of a CLAN initiated attack. He had already instructed his closest generals to prepare for a massive conflict.

But it would not come to that; a referendum to go to war with the CLAN was approved in the house, giving Chief Ukama full power to lead the conglomerate in this great war.

27
Emergency is Declared

Things moved fast once the CERS assembly passed the referendum giving the commander in chief full authorization to initiate war. The chief declined a public address, but his communications office released a short note to the media.

"The people of CERS have declared a level 2 emergency in light of the CLAN's recent incursions and spying attacks. As a universal power, we reserve the right to protect the sovereignty of our great conglomerate. We are willing to do everything required to keep our people safe."

A few hours after this release, the CLAN also declared a level 2 in response. Within the span of a day, the Milky Way was pushed to the verges of the most grievous conflict it had seen yet.

28
CLAN Readies for the War
The Presidential House, Capital District of the CLAN.

"Kvazim President, we are monitoring the situation around the clock. We have assembled our corps on an unprecedented scale at strategic locations. Our forces are ready to respond in kind against any act of war. But, as you know, it is a stalemate situation along the frontier."

Hermip Iyo, Chief of the CLAN's Spatial Security Force, addressed the president as he stood at the head of the table. A massive zereal screen displayed a map of the Milky Way behind him. Also in attendance were Senator Jebbmy, all three of the President's advisers, senior ministers, and the army chiefs. They'd been butting heads since the early morning hours. It was almost lunchtime now, and the quiet ones were getting restless.

"How much do we know of their strategy?" Zxea asked the chief.

"Per our simulations, they might push along the perimeter's western side." The general pointed to a region on the screen.

"Why there? Is that a weak spot for us?"

"If we go by their perception, then yes," the chief replied, "Nevertheless, we have bolstered our defenses in that area over the past few years. It was one of the key recommendations to come out of the T55 conflict. This, of course, remains classified information. They will get trapped if they come through the western corridor."

"Mm-hmm." Zxea nodded and then said, "What about the neutral clusters?"

"We're good in clusters 1 through 5, except for the nation of Priscia." The general continued using all of his six feet two inches to tower over the gathering. "They refuse to accept any military protection."

The chief then went on to explain the buildup of CLAN forces surrounding the neutral clusters. As per the Galactic Convention, protecting the neutral clusters within CLAN space in the event of a conflict was the CLAN's responsibility.

"I am concerned with the increased political activity in Priscia," Rofix Dejo, minister for political affairs, chimed in. He'd pointedly looked at the small planet's shimmering form. "According to our intel, their Riok is assembling a third front of the neutral planets."

"Yes, I have heard those murmurs too. Is he getting any traction - also, what is our exposure?" Zxea turned her head to Rofix.

"Surprisingly, yes. The Riok, his real name is Kinmuk, by the way, has created quite a buzz among the neutrals. They are all rallying around him. He is an influential chap, in a non-political way."

"Well, that's ironic, isn't it?" Jebbmy spoke out of turn, his palms turned up, shoulders thrust into the neck.

"Indeed," Rofix continued, "And to answer the second part of your question, Kvazim President, we are yet to do a full assessment. I will appraise you as soon as I have a better picture."

"The Riok," General Zima, head of the CLAN's nuclear arsenal, scowled, "Has been yapping moronically about the immorality of war. I am surprised people are even interested in this scam. Those Priscians are not normal people if you ask me." Zima looked too comfortable in his seat. Both legs spread apart, hands encroaching on another chair.

"General Zima," Jebbmy cut off the general before he could add further insult to injury, "Everyone has a right to political opinions. You may ridicule them, but you cannot write them off. I fear this third front will cut into the influence of conglomerates. We may need to make some adjustments for them in the future. But it's nothing you haven't seen already, is it, General? New alliances are formed, and the batons of power exchange hands. That is how the universe works."

"Thanks for the schooling, Senator," the general said, his lip pulled up on one side.

"But I give zero importance to their anti-war diatribe. War, you see, is not inherently bad. If you look at history closely, wars have brought significant progress into human life. And besides, nations are not protected by empty peace rhetoric. That's just wishful thinking. Democracies run on the foundation of stable militaries - they always have."

"Well, so much for academia. Can we focus on the issues at hand here? We are getting hungry; it's been four hours now." Senator Kaqman cringed from a corner.

"I agree with you," Soby Taep, minister for arts and culture, said. "We do not have to resolve the universe in a session, do we now?"

Zxea shook her head in absolute disbelief. Jebbmy smiled at her.

Ye hungry bastards! he felt the urge to shout but resisted. He thought it to be unwise, considering his reputation.

Sitting across from Jebbmy, General Zima was in no hurry for his lunch either. He had stuffed a bunch of pancakes with maple syrup that morning. His chef had resurrected this breakfast delicacy from the twenty-first century by conducting exhaustive research.

"I think we are committing a blunder here, Kvazim President. We know the CERS's arsenal was purpose-built to destroy us. We face a grave danger to our very existence," he said.

"What are you trying to say, General Zuma?" Zxea asked. It was a rhetorical question. She knew what Zima was getting at.

"We should make the first move, choose a weak spot, and hit the enemy hard." The general blurted out in haste. His hands shuffled and waved as he spoke.

This time, it was Jebbmy's turn to speak, even though it was not his area of expertise. "We have traditionally followed a *no first strike* policy, Kvazim President. Engaging in a proactive strike would mean we deviate from it. It seems reckless to start a war when it could easily be avoided through negotiations."

"No first strike," Zxea rubbed the bridge of her nose, "Will still be our credo. Under no circumstance are we to fire that first bullet. We're not the ones seeking this war anyways."

"In that case, our defense strategy has to be foolproof," General Zima leaned forward, putting his forearms on the table in a readied position.

"Which it is - unless you are implying otherwise; we have already heard the chief reiterate that," Jebbmy said.

"But there is always that very tiny chance of an error," Senator Leqo felt it was prudent to speak at this juncture.

"Bingo, you prove my point, Senator Leqo!" Zima quickly piggybacked, "No first strike is not a viable strategy. It makes us sitting ducks. What if the enemy finds our Achilles heel, if we have any, of course - which we may very well, unbeknownst of us."

"Ok, no need to jump ahead, General Zima," Iyo was obviously irritated.

"Our defense is impeccable. We can observe, orient, decide, and act per the situation. Also, we are not planning to sit idle exactly- other strategies will be deployed. Economic embargoes and such, but that's the wider discourse. Anyways, the point is all our units are ready, waiting on orders." Iyo was thorough in his response, his hands moving with the pace of his words, cutting and slicing the air as he spoke.

"Thank you, Chief Iyo," Zxea said. Then she turned with her chair to General Zima and said, "I expect nothing less from the arsenal."

Zima squirmed. The hardliner in him was dying to use the latest cool toys in his arsenal.

"Yes, Kvazim President," he responded, unwillingly.

"And I hope things are good with our operations on H33. It makes me uncomfortable."

"H33 is the jewel in our crown, Kvazim President," said Zima, "And our base there remains a closely guarded secret, even after decades of operations."

"Yes, that, there is my precise worry, General," Zxea replied, her hand pointing in the air, as if H33 hung in front of them like a trinket ball. "My administration has had to inherit it unwillingly."

She then looked at Jebbmy, "Senator, I am not comfortable with our people left vulnerable like that in the neutral zone. I most certainly want to decommission that base once we are out of this mess."

Zima spoke before Jebbmy could, "That may be a little difficult, Kvazim President. In my capacity as the CLAN's arsenal chief, I wish to formally object to any such plan." He breathed heavily as he spoke.

"I appreciate your views, General. But it is not your decision to take." Zxea said tersely. Then she looked around the room, "I hope that is clear to all. Let us never forget we are here to serve the people of the CLAN."

"But Kvazim," Zima was about to say something when Chief Iyo stopped him mid-sentence, touching his shoulder and shaking his head. Zima threw his hands up in the air and leaned back in his chair.

"I understand opinions are involved here, but several other issues are at hand, such as civilian preparedness. Why don't we pace ourselves a little better," Iyo said.

"I concur with you, Chief," Jebbmy liked how the chief had steered clear of Zima. General Zima was known to aggressively hijack discussions to suit his personal agendas.

"Civilian preparedness," said Zxea, "Will be done under Senator Jebbmy's oversight,"

"Shouldn't that be us, Kvazim President," Larico, the minister for food and agriculture, raised her hand like a student asking a question.

"Of course," Zxea replied, not without noticing the condescending tone Larico had taken, "What would we do without your support? But you must involve the senator with you in this work. He brings a wealth of experience in crisis management."

Larico and Zxea were former batchmates at the Academy of Political Science. Both had risen fast through the ranks, and Larico was seen as tough competition to Zxea until Zxea became the President. But Larico certainly did not feature in Zxea's laundry list of worries today.

Zxea got up, straightened her suit, and looked at the congregation in the room.

"This is probably the biggest crisis of our time, folks. We need to be on our toes. I want all departments on high alert. Cancel all leaves, have no other plans. Pay attention to your Vabakas," she paused momentarily and then said, "And for Zumt's sake, have some breakfast before you go to meetings!"

29
Ghirnot Colludes with the CERS

Planet K000-9, Neutral Zone 1.

Chaliza had spun off a fiber dome for Ghirnot and his guest to sit and talk. People still preferred to meet in person for important conversations.

"What's in it for you, though?" Kimnabav asked Ghirnot as she shuffled in her chair, her arms never opening up.

She was uneasy seeing Ghirnot. He had reached out to her out of the blue with a proposal. Apart from the fact that he was a sworn enemy of President Zxea, she did not know much about him.

"Power. Presidency. Revenge." Ghirnot spat the words out one after another, punctuating them each on their own. He wanted to keep this conversation brief. As a politician, he was well aware of the perils that arose from excessive talking.

"But why in that order?" Kimnabav persisted in her questioning. "Retribution ought to be at the top of your list. After all, the president did throw you in a dungeon, didn't she?"

"That she did. But I wouldn't blame her too much." Ghirnot had a wicked smile on his face.

"In her position, I would have done the same. We are all ruthless people, Kvazim. Besides, power is my revenge."

Kimnabav clearly was not satisfied with that answer as she questioned him further, "What about your allegiance to the conglomerate? Don't you think you are betraying your own people?"

"I am not!" Ghirnot said as he jerked his neck. "If anything, I am serving the CLAN and her people by doing this. President Zxea is bad news for my people."

"I'm all ears," Kimnabav uncrossed her arms and leaned forward. She seemed willing to consider the possibility.

Ghirnot observed the change in her demeanor. He held both his hands in front of him like a bowl full of precious coins, and said, "Here's the deal. I can clearly see that you are next in line to become the commander in chief of the CERS. I want to extend a hand of friendship. I would rather have a friend across the aisle."

He knows a good deal about us - enough to be dangerous. Kimnabav was not one to be flattered easily.

"We cannot predict the future now, can we, senator?" She responded after a moment, looking straight up into the eyes of Ghirnot.

"I get that," Ghirnot responded, shrinking his shoulders. "But politics is a game of possibilities. And I know you cannot get to the chair unless Ukama steps down or is impeached. And from what I know of him, he will not abdicate on his own."

"I do not want to be too aspirational here, Senator." Kimnabav was back to her stoic nature, her face incredibly placid. "The CERS chief is not a lightweight by any means. It would need to be a scandal of monolithic proportions to dethrone him."

She looked at a washed-out orange vase on the mahogany desk.

"That's vintage," Ghirnot said, pointing at the vase. "Chaliza here managed to hustle it out for us from Chandrama."

Chaliza was happy at being noticed, "It's vintage earthen, 19th century AD."

"Noted, nice job," Kimnabav said, half yawning, "I have closely looked into the chief, but I haven't found anything significant or proportionately damaging."

"There!" Ghirnot exclaimed, pointing his index finger in the air "Proportionate is the key word here. I have just the right size scandal that would get you what you need."

"I hope you know what you are talking about, Senator." Kimnabav shrugged. "Like I said, I need something big."

"And you are right, Kvazim," Ghirnot replied, leaning forward. "You wouldn't find anything on him. The chief has been, how should I say this – smart enough to stay clean close to home. But I have enough dirt on him. This is about the mining scandal involving planet BVIOP 1."

"Interesting. Isn't that a planet in the neutral zone?" Kimnabav asked.

"It is, which kind of hides it from the glare of your media. You must have heard of the now infamous mining firm Thexacorp. Turns out Ukama had large stakes in it. The money was channeled through Kitgobx, the chief's son-in-law."

"Ah-ha, Kitgobx. I guess that figures." Kimnabav looked away, wondering how she missed this angle. "He has been absent from the scene off and on."

"Smart fellow, this Kitgobx is. Stays out of the limelight. Once the scandal was unearthed, he quietly shifted his operations elsewhere. I have enough evidence to implicate him and the chief. If you are interested, that is."

"What's it going to cost me?" She asked.

"Nothing!" Ghirnot was quick to assume a noble position, posturing benevolence. "Like I said, I would much rather have a friend across the aisle once the power dynamic shifts."

"Let me make one thing clear, Senator." Kimnabav hated false magnanimity. "You are doing this voluntarily. Even if this information proves useful, I owe you nothing."

"Crystal clear, Kvazim," Ghirnot said as he gestured to Chaliza.

Chaliza promptly flew the files to Kimnabav's Vabaka.

"Would you mind boxing that vase for me, please?" Kimnabav said without particularly addressing either of the two.

"Of course, Kvazim! The pleasure is all ours!"

30

A War Brews

A popular news network, Northern Milky Way.

Commoners were not sure what was happening along the frontier and behind the closed doors of the two main powerhouses. They depended on news sources to know, and *Laser News* was one such popular news medium with quirky hosts and expert panelists who seemed to know it all.

***

"How prepared do you think we are for this war?" Kideii asked from the perch of her polished woxbi table. That was the rage these days, expensive wood imported from Planet Ulma. She read from a zereal screen that was used to prompt the anchors, provide them with ideas and news flashes. The host, as well as panelists, sat on tall designer chairs that, at times, made it difficult for the occupants to shift behind, searching for a backrest.

"That is not an easy question to answer," Movsy said. He was a retired Colonel turned defense analyst who was not envious of his previous position now. "These are massive enterprises. Each with enough firepower to destroy one another. My sources tell me half a million Turbo Sparrows stand deployed along the frontier as we speak.

They man the entire border of the CLAN, except maybe for a few barren regions no one cares about. But that's just the sparrows, the leaner opportunistic fighter vehicles. My count could vary a bit, but about two hundred thousand T-rexes are ready to take off at a minute's notice. Besides, those are just the major ones. We possess hundreds of thousands of Space Tanks, Rhuton guns, Hexa Propellers, and whatnot."

"And what about the wave propeller, the famed ultra-damage weapon?" Kideii asked.

"I was coming to that. The wave propellers, also known as planet killers, are not to be used unless it's a doomsday scenario. Let's not talk about that. I do not know enough of them - they make me uncomfortable."

"Them?" Kideii asked, "Do you mean to say we have more than one of these gigantic propellers?"

"Could be, I don't know. I did not have sufficient clearance to know more," Movsy shrugged.

"But that brings me to the next question. What is this war going to cost the citizens of the galaxy - how many people will have to die? If we look back into the past, the first intra - galactic war caused three million casualties, besides destroying scores of terrestrial planets."

"Not to forget the nuclear zones that emerged – multiple space routes were permanently closed. God knows what happened to the colonies beyond those," Riffplo, the co-host of the TV show, chimed in. The talkative counterpart to Kideii, he wore a permanent half smile that was supposed to set their audience at ease.

"That is beyond me, honestly. I am just a retired soldier. You can ask me about weapons and war strategies and such – but please do not ask me of human avarice. No one knows what it costs," Movsy replied in the same way he usually spoke, like a grandparent reading a bedtime story, soft and unassuming.

"Hmmm." Riffplo sighed, then said, "Let us talk about those strategies now. What do you make of the stand-off on the frontier? Do you think the CERS will attack first? Or will it be us?"

"Let us try and analyze what has happened till now, shall we?" Movsy said. It was a rhetorical question. In his mind, he wanted to go over the events and make sense of them for himself. In reality, he was as perplexed as anyone else.

"Things first got out of hand when one of our code vehicles accidentally entered the CERS's sanctum sanctorum. President Zxea was quick to clarify this was a mere accident and nothing else. And it appears, like I said before, that the Commander-in-Chief Ukama of the CERS was willing to let this one slide. But he was pressured into action by his coalition partners. For them, this incursion was enough for the CERS to declare an emergency and put its forces on a level 2 alert."

"Would you mind telling us what this alert means, Colonel Movsy?" Riffplo asked.

"For sure. A level 2 alert is basically a signal to prepare for war. If I were to oversimplify, it means the war starts tomorrow, brace yourself."

"Thank you, Colonel," said Kideii, finding a chance to re-enter the conversation, "Please continue," she said.

Riffplo was not pleased with this little encroachment, the barest hint of a grimace that was quickly covered flashed, but he remained quiet. The two hosts tended to compete with each other at every possible opportunity. Their competition was part of the appeal and popularity of the show.

"Yes. So, when your archrival declares a level 2 alert, you are not left with any options but to follow suit. So did we."

"But why do you think President Zxea's efforts to de-escalate failed?" Riffplo jumped right back in.

"Hmmm. We must understand how the political dynamic is shifting on both sides as this storm gathers on the frontier." Movsy took a pause. Staring into a limbo, he continued "I hear the hardliners, the Cabal in particular, is trying to topple over Chief Ukama. I have heard of similar efforts happening from within the CLAN as well. A large swathe of senators wants President Zxea gone."

"Is that because she is a woman? For Zumt's sake, it's the seventh millennium," Kideii interrupted exasperatingly.

I can't believe she is bringing this angle now. What a show-off! Riffplo grumbled inaudibly.

"That does not seem to be the case here. President Zxea is a very strong leader. She has kept her opponents, mainly Senator Ghirnot and his friends, subdued for the past four years with an iron fist. That is not a mean task." Movsy said. "What is happening with her now is typical of what happens to popular leaders who are strong and in full control. They pave their own path to destruction."

"How do you mean, Colonel?" Riffplo asked, "Are you referring to the mistrial of Senator Ghirnot?"

"Yes, that and this whole security lapse. The mistrial was a political blunder. If it were up to me, I would have fired the advisers first and then this Marxzib fellow. It was – what they used to call in ancient times – a political Hara-kiri".

"Please explain!" Riffplo said, "We know what the term means, but many may not."

"It was a ritual suicide practiced by Samurai warriors in ancient times. Anyways, I think President Zxea pretty much walked herself into this mess".

"You said you would have fired her advisers, and someone called Marxzib. Would you talk more on this, I'm hearing this name for the first time," said Riffplo.

"Well, I spoke too much there. I shouldn't have said any names. But Zumt – who cares anymore? It's common grapevine. He was heading the team that messed up with the horse."

"That's interesting. Tell us more on this, please, Colonel," Riffplo prodded him.

"I would love to, when I know more about him," Movsy said, "Anyways, it seemed for a time that Chief Ukama was willing to buy the claim, that this entire "horse" thing was an accident and was willing to ignore it. But he was put under immense pressure to give a fitting and stern response by the general public, hawks within his administration, and of course you people – the media."

"Why would you count us among them, Colonel? We are CLAN" Kideii retorted sharply.

"Are you now, I thought the media was supposed to be neutral?" Movsy scoffed.

Kideii gave a tight-lipped smile and then steered away from the conversation. "Can you tell us more about the Cabal?"

"Well, well. The whole thing started as a think tank. It was to work as a pressure group keeping a tab on the administration – especially when it came to the interests of the privileged classes. But as time went on, the Cabal became increasingly powerful within the CERS. Soon they were influencing major decisions within the capital and at times tinkered with the government."

"Who do they represent, though – what do you mean when you say, privileged classes?" Riffplo asked.

"So, the CERS went through great social upheavals over the last two millennia. People who were up in the social ladder went down. The Bilkpir people, who had emerged as the ruling social elite during the fifth millennium, were gradually replaced by others in all walks of life. The Cabal rose as a pressure group to safeguard the interests of the Bilkpirs. But if you ask me, it's the money they were after. Their ideologies simply present a façade to this entity. There are some brilliant businesspeople dictating everything from behind the curtain. My guess is that chief Ukama wants to control the mining trade throughout the CERS through a slew of shell companies run by his son-in-law. The Cabal, on the other hand, wants the Bilkpir business folk to extract this pound of flesh from-"

At this, Riffplo stopped him and then addressed the screen "At this point, we want to appraise our viewers of the emerging situation within the CERS capital. It has come to light that Chief Ukama has been implicated in a mining scandal involving his son-in-law and a few other influential ministers from his cabinet."

He then turned to the Colonel again, "Apologies for the interruption, Colonel, please continue."

"Well, that's where we are now. It's basically a standoff. Forces are waiting to proceed on both sides, but the politics have turned precarious. If I were to predict, we might see major leadership changes in the CLAN pretty soon."

"But what about the war? Do you think we will see a full-fledged conflict?"

"I can't predict the future. But the odds are low. I am hoping the sane ones will de-escalate the situation for everyone's sake."

31

A Standoff

Planet K000-9, Neutral Zone 1.

NIHOLI KIRIPTOF, AMBASSADOR OF the CLAN, had invited Ambassador Pixi, the longest-serving CERS ambassador, for an urgent meeting. Kiriptof's staff had spun off a twenty-second-century post-modern ambiance for their globe on K000-9. These were difficult times. A war was brewing between the two conglomerates, and level two emergencies had been declared from both sides. Kiriptof thought it would be a change of scenery to meet someplace quiet, away from the increasingly stressful air of the capital.

"Ambassador, thank you for agreeing to see me on such short notice. President Zxea and her administration are thankful to you." Kiriptof shook hands with Pixi.

"Pleasure," Pixi replied with a loose handshake, "I guess I had to come. Despite the shenanigans from your beloved administration, believe me, it's always a pleasure to see an old friend." Pixi quickly assumed a high moral ground since the CLAN had erred this time. It was the usual game of power-pong these two had subscribed to. You never knew who would have the upper hand.

Kiriptof did not respond right away, instead, he signaled the ambassador to sit.

"I am fine, thank you." Pixi refused plainly. He'd decided to appear not friendly today. Pixi was known to be too nice and a pushover at times. However, with the war looming large on the horizon, he had no choice but to come across strong. Kiriptof half smiled, probably realizing Pixi's dilemma, and offered him Timiltan whiskey instead, which Pixi gladly accepted.

"You know it was an accident. Nothing deliberate. We are the CLAN, for Zumt's sake; we don't even prosecute our criminals." Kiriptof said.

"You don't?"

"No, we don't. We simply send them to remote colonies with some restrictions. Tell me now, how can we, a hyper-liberal state, want a war with you, Pixi?"

Pixi shrugged. *Whatever*.

"Care to explain what your folks were doing in our domain?" Pixi asked "There is a red line in terms of our sovereignty. The CLAN, I am afraid, has crossed that line. Now we do not have any option but to enforce our military might."

"Some strong words there, my respected colleague." Kiriptof said, "But I assume you must have heard President Zxea's speech this morning. We most certainly do not advocate any hostility toward the CERS. What happened was an unfortunate occurrence. The administration is working with our analyst community to put controls in place to avoid any such events in the future," Kiriptof tried to downplay the incursion.

"Occurrence!" Pixi scoffed. "It was an incursion for Zumt's sake. This whole rhetoric of "accidental occurrence" is wearing me out. I would have expected you to express at least some regret. But I do not see you heading there any soon. How am I to believe any word you're saying."

"We believe," Kiriptof placed his glass down with a heavy thud on the table, "We are within our rights to safeguard our galactic interests.

As we have brought to your attention on several occasions in the past - there have been similar attempts from your side as well."

"I am not sure what attempts you're referring to. Our analysts perform regular scans and security checks. But never have we even once encroached into your zone, nor did we steal your property." Pixi stood his ground.

"We haven't stolen any of your possessions, Ambassador. The accidental," he cleared his throat, "Data asset was duly destroyed per our intra-galactic security and compliance conventions. Having said that, we must forget and forgive. Let bygones be bygones. We at CLAN believe in a shared future for the residents of the Milky Way. And that in that future - there is no place for a war."

"Does that glorious, shared future of yours include spying? Sabotage? Covert operations, perhaps?" Pixi took some barbed swipes. The whiskey had undoubtedly helped him.

"I get that you are angry, Pixi. But believe me, given our power dynamic, such a slip could have happened on anyone's side. It was merely incidental that it happened through one of ours."

"A theft is never coincidental, Ambassador Kiriptof. And besides, we cannot ignore the fundamental folly here. The public is agitated; they think we are scared of you guys. The commander in chief is under pressure to act tough. He is struggling to rebuild the confidence people had in him once."

"I understand," Kiriptof said, "Let me ask you this. What can we possibly do to make things easier for you? We, as a team, need to de-escalate this situation. And more than that," Kiriptof put his hand on Pixi's shoulder, "What can I do to speed things up?"

"Well, for starters, the people of CERS would like to see a clean-cut apology from the head of your state. Own up to the lapse and say sorry. And yes, there is no team here, not after what you have done."

"You ask for too much, Pixi." Kiriptof brought his hand down, picking his glass back up to swallow the rest, his Adam's apple bobbing as he downed it before pouring another tumbler full. "It would be political suicide for the president to call it a lapse, as it happened under her watch. No sitting head of a state can publicly acknowledge a mistake and not face the consequences."

"Sitting - that's the key word here," Pixi said. "But a newly sworn-in leader can easily own up to their predecessor's mistakes and come out of it unscathed."

"Are you asking the CLAN for-" Kiriptof splashed whiskey on his hand, swearing under his breath. He set down the bottle and grabbed a silk handkerchief. He was clearly taken aback by Pixi's bold suggestion.

"Yes, a sacrifice. If President Zxea is made to resign, the incoming president can simply blow over this cloud. And then you and I can both go back to our respective homes and relax. I hate this tension. Something's got to give." Pixi said, casually taking a seat and sipping from his own mostly full glass.

"I am a mere bureaucrat, Pixi. I do not hold that kind of sway in our political alleyways."

"Well, I know someone who does. Why don't you see Senator Leqo and Senator Kaqman? They might have some solution to your political problem."

"Wait a minute, Pixi - how do you know these guys? They are hardly influential. I certainly did not expect you to be in bed with them."

"That is not important, my friend. The clear and present problem on our hands right now is to avoid this bloody war. Chief Ukama does not wish to start a brawl with you guys at this juncture. But he would have no choice if the CLAN won't budge."

Kiriptof shook his head, partly in disbelief, partly in frustration.

"I will see what I can do, Ambassador Pixi. But no promises."

"Understood, Ambassador. Until then, our forces must play this staring contest on the frontiers. It's a standoff for now."

32
A Scandal is Out in the Open
A strumcast show, Southern Milky Way.

"Some of our viewers may find it disturbing, but the truth about the reckless destruction of Qanet BVIOP 1 is now out in the open, and from what I'm seeing, this does not look good." Rtuolip Swqxi, the show host of the popular strumcast "CERS now," spoke grimly. Rtuolip was not unlike the newscasters on the other side of the galaxy, he was talkative, usually smiling, and he knew how to face the Praxima-prompter and give his best angles. Something he was still doing even in the face of tragedy.

"As we all know, the Qanet was rendered unlivable due to excessive mining on its surface. It took a massive humanitarian effort to evacuate three hundred thousand people from the Qanet to neighboring planets."

"This crisis was an eye-opener. We all know what happened to our ultimate motherland, the beautiful planet Earth. Conservationists have warned us against precisely such human-made calamities for thousands of years. However, our politicians and business folks have not learned anything from our past."

"We have a special guest with us tonight, noted galactic conservation activist Blixipi, to talk about this crisis. Blixipi, as some of you already know, is respected for her monumental efforts in getting multiple oil refineries and illegal Migbodium mines closed. Blixipi, who refuses to use a last name, has faced much hatred and ridicule from the business lobbies over the past years - but she refuses to relent. She is like a breath of fresh air in this atmosphere polluted with corporate and political avarice. Welcome to the show, Blixipi!"

Rtuolip flashed a bright smile turning only slightly in his seat for the interview. Across from him was a fragile-looking young woman with her hands firmly planted in her lap to keep her from fidgeting.

She tried to smile as she said, "Thank you, Rtuolip. I must thank you for your continual efforts in holding politicians to account; I am happy to be here."

"The pleasure's all mine, Blixipi. Talk to us about BVIOP 1. It is quite a tragedy, isn't it?"

"It is, indeed, a human-made travesty. The Qanet, to begin with, has been a poor economic region. When the corporations entered, people hoped the situation would change. The mines would bring new jobs and new businesses. However, the reverse happened. At the time of the evacuation, BVIOP 1 was even poorer than before. Locals did not get any of the promised benefits. Majority of the work was done with machines, and there were fewer jobs to be had, most of which were taken by outsiders flown in for their technical expertise."

Blixipi took a pause looking down at her hands before continuing, "The initial discoveries fueled a mad race for exploratory excavations throughout the Qanet. Hundreds of farming families were relocated from their agricultural lands to urban areas. Most ended up giving their precious lands for meager prices. The local politicians and mafias made a killing in this. But the poor suffered. The corporations moved them to ghettos with no land to cultivate and zero employment opportunities to make a living."

"Didn't the local government intervene?"

"Well, they did a decent job initially. And it is quite possible some locals may have benefitted from the mines, but the overall numbers are frightening. Besides, Thexacorp - the culprit-in-chief here, ran hundreds of smaller mines under the guise of artisanal mines."

"What is an artisanal mine?"

"It was basically a provision to protect the financial interests of the local people. The idea was that the locals would run their artisanal mines in the allocated area and benefit from it financially. The place was so rich in Migbodium that even a simple operation could yield several pounds of the mineral."

"Sounds perfect, so what went wrong?"

"Well, Thexacorp spun off hundreds of smaller mines and ran their operations all across the region. Thexacorp registered mines in the locals' names in return for small weekly rent payments. As it happened, these mini mines were bled dry within a matter of weeks, so all the owners could make was a few weeks' worth of rent while Thexacorp ran away with thousands of pounds of the mineral."

"That is appalling,"

"It is. And mind you, Thexacorp ran five of its mega mines too. These mines ultimately proved to be fatal to the region."

"Fatal how?"

"Thexacorp first began drilling using the Cyanide extraction process, an archaic way of extracting minerals. The good-meaning residents of the Earth had banned this process at the end of the third millennium for environmental reasons. Thexacorp, for some reason, re-invented many old processes."

"I can comment on that," Rtuolip glanced off camera then back to the prompter as the information was flashed to him, "It is becoming a pattern these days for illegal activities. Corporations tend to use older methods, which are hard to detect - as against the contemporary methods which leave an audit trail everywhere, very easy to detect."

"That could very well be it," Blixipi nodded in agreement. "Thexacorp first exploited the lands to get the Migbodium out and then kept digging for the large deposits of Earthanium and Glycera. Each of these mines discharged hundreds of millions of tons of tailings."

"*Tailing* - what on Zumt does that mean? It sounds like a bad thing the way you say it."

"Well, it is bad for the environment for sure. *Tailing* is the toxic sludge that comes from the mines. Once the valuable metal is extracted from the soil, much waste is left over. It can potentially contain toxic chemicals, heavy metals, and even radioactive agents. Thexacorp used large earthen embankments called dams to store this sludge."

"Wait a minute, they actually stored the toxin?"

"Yes. These dams cause a foul odor in the surrounding areas and contaminate the nearby soil and water. It is a highly unsafe practice still in use after thousands of years. Unfortunately for BVIOP 1, several of these dams broke off when it was hit with a minor earthquake, and the Tailings flooded into the region. That is when the evacuation efforts, led by the CLAN's President, were swung into action."

"The president did a good job with it, didn't she?"

"Yes, and I thought she deserved a Jeeble prize for the effort, but that is a different story. Anyways, the CLAN rescue was able to save about three hundred thousand people. However, it is estimated that the deluge killed two hundred thousand people. Most died due to the toxic effects. "

"That makes it the largest humanitarian disaster in the millennium, right?"

"Yes, it does, but it doesn't end there. The devastation continued after people had left. The abandoned mines got flooded with rainwater, causing a deluge of acid drains and toxic sludge into rivers and streams. Soon, organisms in the reservoirs started dying, followed by the large animals in the area. Long seasons of drought followed the initial rainfall. Eventually, the forests on the Qanet gave away and basically dried out."

"I do not know what to say. I am speechless."

"It was a big disaster. Some scientists have estimated the Qanet may need another five centuries for the toxic effects to wane."

Both were silent for a moment after this.

"This is the universe we live in, folks," Rtuolip said in a somber tone, shaking and bobbing his head in disbelief, "This is the universe. And it does not stop with pillaging our planets; it continues from there, by misusing our money," he emphasized, "Taxpayer's money to fuel these evil enterprises."

"I agree with you there, Rtuolip," Blixipi said, "In the wake of this scandal if I am allowed to use that word, we must demand the commander in chief resigns. He and his accomplices must be brought to justice. There is no way this abomination should fall on the heads of innocent people of the CERS."

"Precisely. Whoever leaked the evidence also made it available to the general public. I, for one, have looked at the evidence closely - now, I am not a lawyer, but the nexus of shell firms clearly points to Kitgobx."

"Yes. It was done cleverly. On the face of it, the firm Thexacorp has no clear owner. But if you follow the trail of the hundreds of shell firms listed, it finally leads to Kitgobx. He has allegedly made something to the tune of five Quantixos through multiple deals over the five years in question. The sheer scale of this scam - that's the right word for it - is staggering. There is no way he could have pulled this on his own. Kitgobx must have had backing, political or otherwise."

"We all know who is behind this. It is clear as daylight," Rtuolip spoke confidently in the manner of an intrepid journalist. "The opposition is rallying for Chief Ukama's resignation. It would take some miracle for the chief to survive a scandal of these proportions."

33

MATTERS OF CONFIDENCE

Headquarters of the Torial Party, Jikgea, the Capital of CERS. Southern Milky Way.

THE CERS'S ASSEMBLY HAD a two-way split. The Torial party, led by Uxcy Civorxta, and the Democrats, led by Charbes Koya. The Torials had come to power after a hiatus of fifteen years. Before that, the CERS was led by a charming democrat, Torin Ura, almost single-handedly. Ura was extremely popular with the people, especially the ones in their thirties and above. During his tenure, the Torials had realized they had no option but to wait for him to either make some political blunder or die. The former never happened, but the latter did. The Torials took over the assembly with an absolute majority as an aftereffect.

The power equation within the CERS was highly polarized. Civorxta controlled the party, while Chief Ukama controlled the administration. Each had their unique work style and were popular within their spheres of influence. Two years ago, when the Torials entered the assembly with an absolute majority, Civroxta supported Ukama for the commander in chief position, taking a back seat owing to her domestic priorities. However, as time passed, Civorxta had started becoming increasingly restless with the chief's ever-growing clout. He had managed to keep her out of the loop for critical governance matters, including the current tensions with the CLAN.

When a small media outlet called "*Blastz*" released the news of Chief Ukama's alleged involvement in the pillaging of planet BVIOP, Civorxta naturally took this as an opportunity to uproot Ukama from his coveted chair.

On the third day after the news broke, Civorxta released an intra-party no-confidence notice against Chief Ukama to the sitting Torial members. The notice read as follows:

> *"The Torial party abides by the high ethical and moral standards laid down by our proud founders. Recent allegations involving Commander in Chief Ukama have cast serious questions on the current administration and, indeed, on the chief. Many of you have personally contacted me over the past couple of days and raised grave concerns.*
>
> *As the elected representatives of this hallowed assembly, we owe it to the people of the CERS that we maintain integrity in running their government. The unfortunate events over the past few days have done irreversible damage to our image and shaken the confidence of the good people of this conglomerate.*
>
> *As the leader of this great party, I am filing a no-confidence motion against Chief Ukama. All elected members are asked to convene in the CERS headquarters to vote on the motion. The date and time shall be conveyed to you soon.*
>
> *I expect the honorable members to consider the well-be-*

ing of our people and respect our glorious traditions of trust, honesty, and integrity while making a decision.

A copy of this notice has also been shared with the honorable speaker Koply Wornot per the agreed conventions of the assembly."

Civorxta took advantage of an obscure provision from the party bylaws in releasing this notice. Per the provision, a party president was allowed to bring in a no-confidence vote against a party-native commander in chief under exceptional circumstances, with the due approval from five top-ranking party officials. Most of the current ranking officials in the party were handpicked by Civorxta; they had no qualms in approving her request, especially under the guise of overwhelming public outcry against the chief.

34

A Coup Brews

The Cabal Quarters, Jikgea, the Capital of CERS. Southern Milky Way.

The Cabal was not a political party. It was a school of thought that ran like an undercurrent of the Torial party, an organization within another. Formed some three hundred years ago, this think tank represented extreme conservatism bordering on lines of hatred. Many in the Torial party found them too hawkish to tolerate. Much to the frustration of its leaders, consecutive party chiefs in the recent past had kept the Cabal on the fringe, using it only when convenient.

Kimnabav was everything the Cabal could have wished for in a leader. A Doctor of Philosophy in political science, Kimnabav was an aggressive orator and an able organizer. With Ukama's ship in the doldrums, she seemed to be only a stone's throw away from the much sought-after post.

***

"This has to be it; we must drag him down, now." Kimnabav was clearly agitated. She was pacing up and down the room as she spoke with the top leaders of the Cabal.

"How do you mean?" Kiquib squinted his eyes with skepticism.

"It's a serious scandal; the whole of the Milky Way is talking about it. It is also our best opportunity to throw him over." Kimnabav said, her words tumbling out in a rush.

"Never! Never, ever!" Kiquib slammed his fist on the massive Hikarop table. "Chief Ukama has been a friend. We cannot possibly backstab him." Kiquib was a long-time Cabal loyalist and an Ukama sympathizer. He liked to think of the chief as a friend. For others in the Cabal, he was merely one of the several court jesters the chief had gathered around him for wine and dine soirees.

"Your friend?" Nibkowt retorted sharply, "Ukama is not your friend – he keeps people like you around for entertainment." Nibkowt, another long-time Cabal member, was a staunch supporter of Kimnabav.

"You stay out of this, Nibkowt," Kiquib pointed a finger at Nibkowt, raising his voice with every word.

"Now that we are talking about it," Kimnabav intervened, "I think Nibkowt is right. The Cabal has no friends. We are an organization run on principles. Petty personal relationships mean nothing to us. We must vote against the chief during the no-confidence motion. Also, take the right-wingers with us."

"Petty relationships?" Kiquib snorted, "The guy is your mentor, for Zumt's sake! Have you no regard for decency, Kimnabav?"

"I cannot possibly deal with this emotional blabber, not at this time," Kimnabav shouted in frustration. "There are no friendships at work here - it's a war. A war we have been fighting for all these years. We cannot choke with emotions at the crunch hour. This is our time, our opportunity; we must seize it."

"I agree with you, member Kimnabav," Waqipk said, looking quietly out of the window as the three squabbled. "It's time we took over the reins. You have my full support." Although there was no official hierarchy in the Cabal, Waqipk was considered to be the leader of this group.

"Mine as well," Ewuko, the core council's fifth member, chimed in. Ewuko was the quiet, non-confrontational one within this cohort.

"I am with you as well, member Kimnabav," said Nibkowt.

"I do not condone this approach," Kiquib continued to sulk. "But I am with you, if that's what you all feel is right for the cause." He had probably realized the futility of butting heads with everyone on this issue.

"Ok. We are good then. Let us chalk out the details now." Waqipk said.

Kimnabav nodded in agreement.

For the next half an hour, the group debated a notorious scheme that would lead the Cabal to the ultimate goal its founders had envisioned several centuries ago.

35

THE CHIEF WEIGHS OPTIONS

Office of the Commander in Chief, Jikgea, the Capital of CERS. Southern Milky Way.

"They are trying to squeeze me out. Those cunning bastards."

Chief Ukama paced across the room. His bald head shone bright red under the recently installed clean *fuora* lights. Three of his trusted political advisors, senators Jity, Kimnabav, and Hioma, were in attendance.

"They blindsided us, sir." Said Kimnabav, "I am surprised at how quickly Civorxta brought the motion. The party brass must be under her spell."

Kimnabav crossed her arms in front of her. It was unusual for her to betray such caution. But the chief didn't notice it; he was too angry to think straight.

"Ahem," Feliv Hioma, the quiet one among the three, cleared his throat, "I concur with Kvazim Kimnabav. This is plain and simple sabotage. I suspect Civorxta and her coterie have put in all of their power behind this."

"I bet she has. But we will deal with her later. For now, we must gain support from as many Torials as possible. Kimnabav," the chief turned toward Kimnabav who sat on his left, "You are responsible to round up the right-wingers. Jity," he looked at Jity Khalem, sitting next to Kimnabav, "I trust you with the moderates. Hioma, work with the lawyers and see if we can stall this no-confidence vote. There must be some loophole in the bylaws."

The chief laid out his orders loud and clear.

"But we need a strong pitch, sir. I am afraid the allegations have severely damaged our reputation." Jity said, chewing each word carefully before saying it; he did not want to anger the chief.

"ALLEGATIONS!" The chief slammed his fist on the giant table before him.

"Deny them. Refute them. Trash them. Summon the CERS's top journalists for lunch with me tomorrow. I will personally explain to them how Kitgobx acted on his own. This has nothing to do with me. I haven't seen him in the last six months, for Zumt's sake."

All three knew the chief was lying. But no one said a word. Kimnabav was playing with her fingers, her mind was running at several machs. Jity was looking at the massive roof aimlessly. Hioma, it appeared, was the only one gravely concerned, judging from his furrowed face.

"We may need something stronger than a rebuttal, sir. Something tangible." Hioma added after a long pause.

"Ok." the chief grunted. "I get that. Let's bribe the Zumt out of them. Promise them two hundred irexos each. Throw in fully paid trips to Earth. Do whatever it takes. Threaten them if they don't oblige. I need to see an overwhelming majority come voting day."

"I will get on with the right-wingers, Chief." Kimnabav said. She seemed to have gained her composure back.

"That is good. Listen, folks; I have handed you great careers on a platter here. It is time for you to earn them. Show me you can still do some good for me. Now get on with it. There is no time to lose." the chief growled.

All three disappeared one by one. Chief Ukama was left alone in his sprawling office. He felt the ground slipping fast from beneath his feet.

36

Kimnabav 1, Ukama 0

Office of the Commander in Chief, Jikgea, the Capital of CERS. Southern Milky Way.

Ukama was chugging Zimian whisky from a large tumbler when he was alerted by his Vabaka of an incoming communication. It was Civorxta, his nemesis in chief.

"To what do I owe this pleasure, Kvazim Civorxta?" The chief grunted as he saw her face on the large screen before him.

"How are you doing, Ukama?" The lack of propriety said she still wanted to be a friend.

"Wow. You forgot already that I am still the commander in chief. Such arrogance." The chief responded with a grunt as he filled himself a large portion.

"Why blame me, honorable Commander in Chief? "Civorxta scoffed. "Forgive me, but you brought this on yourself."

"What do you mean? Are you mocking me?"

"I am not the enemy here, so cool down, Chief. Your own people have betrayed you. It was Kimnabav who leaked that report to the media. She has also turned the right-wingers against you. You cannot win the vote without their support. If I were you, I would resign straightway. Save the embarrassment."

"Do you think I am a fool, CIVORXTA?!" The chief shouted. "I know what you are doing here. Kimnabav is my protege; I have practically raised her. She will never betray me." The veins on the side of his head bulged as he spoke.

"Come on, Chief. Wake up. Think rationally." Civorxta wasn't rattled by the chief's temper, but the slight upturn at the corner of her lip let him know she knew she had hit a nerve.

"Aren't you surprised how this thing dropped out of the blue? I have records of Kimnabav meeting secretly with a clan operative on K000-9. I believe it was the infamous Senator Ghirnot, who she met with. He offered her this scandal on a platter."

The chief could not believe what he heard, rather he did not *want* to believe it.

But somehow, her story made a lot of sense. Kimnabav has been acting weird lately. Poor Jity had tried warning him on several occasions, but the chief had dismissed him, thinking Jity was simply acting out of jealousy.

"Listen, Chief. I am handing you an olive branch. Look into what I have told you. I will hold off on the vote for now. Resign quietly and walk away. I will see to it that no charges are brought against you." Civorxta disconnected the line.

A very disturbed chief asked his intelligence head to locate Kimnabav and bring her to him. The officers tried for several hours. Kimnabav was nowhere to be found. They also confirmed that the leak could have possibly come from within his team. The chief knew he had been betrayed - and that his game as the commander in chief of the CERS was over.

37
A New Leader is Born

Jikgea, the capital of CERS. A virtual conference. Southern Milky Way.

Koply Wornot, the speaker of the CERS's assembly, had asked for Kimnabav and Civorxta to join him for an urgent conversation. Chief Ukama had resigned an hour after midnight, and it was the speaker's mandate to find a leader that would replace him and to do it quickly.

"Ok, now that you two are here, let us hear it." Koply said, his voice had a sense of urgency.

"Honorable Speaker, I assure you; we have our party's full support." Kimnabav looked at Civorxta, who was wearing her usual poker face.

Civorxta had no particular liking toward Kimnabav, but that did not bother her, especially at this time. She looked at his whole episode as a stop-gap arrangement.

"Do you concur, Kvazim Civorxta? I sense some hesitation in the room," the speaker asked.

"We have received word of full support from Kvazim Civorxta here, Mr. speaker." Kimnabav jumped right in, not letting the conversation take any unwanted turns.

Civorxta looked unmoved for a few moments. But then said, "Yes, honorable speaker, considering the precarious situation we are in, the members of the Torial party have unanimously decided to extend our support to Kvazim Kimnabav."

"Ok, in that case, congratulations are in order, Kvazim Kimnabav." Koply said as he turned to Kimnabav's screen. "We will soon need to start addressing you as the chief now. We will hold the swearing-in ceremony in my chambers first thing tomorrow morning," he continued in a cheerful voice. "Go on now, break a leg! You have to take over this ship in troubled waters; I wish you well." He said as he disconnected the line.

Kimnabav was relieved and ecstatic. After all, she was going to be known as the youngest commander in chief of the CERS henceforth.

Part Three

Two weeks before the kill shot.

38
How the Heroes Fall

CLAN Headquarters, Capital District of CLAN. Northern Milky Way.

Kaqman was addressing the stability council. The nine-member council was selected through a voting process by the CLAN house. Jebbmy had presided over the vote and saw to it that Kaqman led the council.

"The constitution implies a presiding president must have the confidence of a minimum of sixty percent of the house in order to continue. Our job today is to assess the mood of the house and decide whether or not the president should face a no-confidence vote. Now, I believe each of us has received the mandate from their constituent members, representing the conglomerate."

"Yes."

"Aye,"

"Yeah,"

"That's perfect. Let us put this thing to the vote. Please remember your vote must reflect your constituent members and not your own personal biases. Please start putting your votes in now."

The members obliged. Six out of nine had voted in favor of bringing the no-confidence motion against President Zxea. This is how the official transcript released by the council read:

"The council feels President Zxea has put the conglomerate in harm's way through reckless use of the CLAN's security apparatus. A grave threat of war has arisen before us, and we believe the president must be held accountable for allowing this to happen.

39

DAMAGED GOODS

The Presidential House, Capital District of CLAN. Northern Milky Way.

ZXEA HAD CALLED HER parliamentary affairs minister for an emergency meeting. The damage was done; now was the time to reflect and, pivot, take action as required.

"I need your advice. Mheilia!" Zxea said hurriedly before Mheilia could even close the door of the rotund office on her way in.

"Of course, Kvazim President. How can I help?" Mheilia said as she steadied herself, looking at Zxea, trying to gauge her emotional state. Zxea's voice had urgency but wasn't as sharp as it usually was, which caught Mheilia's attention.

Mheilia was Zxea's closest political confidant and the only person she could consider a friend in the administration.

"Do we need to take some actions internally?"

"I am assuming you are referring to Senator Ghirnot's trial?" Mheilia responded.

"Yes. The whole episode has been an embarrassment. That along with the intelligence failure - or incursion as it is being termed now." Zxea said.

Mheilia hesitated momentarily and then said, "Can I speak freely, Kvazim?"

"Of course. We are just two friends here. And you can call me by my name, Mheilia."

"Thanks, Zxea. It is high time we start holding people accountable for their reckless actions. The optics are important; we need to send out strong messages."

"Yes, but how?"

"Let us start with the trial issue. If you ask me, Zebero and Kamado misled you into believing we had a solid case. Which it clearly wasn't. We could have simply waited and used the dirt on the senator as political leverage."

"Yes." Zxea said as she perched on the edge of the massive desk that served as the centerpiece of the rotund office. "I remember you had concerns. I should have listened to you. This is a brutal game; one error in judgment and the whole universe collapses around me."

This was a surreal moment for Mheilia. She was seeing this side of Zxea for the first time. The otherwise fiery president of the CLAN appeared weak and vulnerable.

Mheilia rose from her chair and walked over to Zxea. Even though it was against the protocol to touch a sitting president, she put her hand on Zxea's shoulder gently.

"I can imagine Zxea. As a leader, you may not have all the facts lined up before you- precisely the reason why people like us are hired as your advisors, to provide you with best possible advice based on facts. But clearly, that has not happened here. This political maneuver has snowballed into a major crisis - and the intelligence lapse has worsened it."

"I get that Mheilia, but it's different with Marxzib. Intelligence is a gray area. I can't blame him or his team; they were only doing their jobs. We expect our analysts to keep trawling space for any possible threats."

"That shouldn't matter. The president of the CLAN is responsible for the well-being of billions of people under their command. At times, they err under pressure. Advisors, analysts, and anyone else working for the government do not have that luxury. I understand Marxzib was doing his job - but he could have been careful. I fail to see what made them touch that Blueprint."

Zxea was feeling conflicted. Her affection for Marxzib meant she protected him at any costs. But it made little sense politically.

"What do you suggest, Mheilia?" She asked as she rubbed her face with her palms.

"Here's what I recommend. All three of them should be relieved of their responsibilities with immediate effect. Specifically," Mheilia moved away and now stood leaning against the desk.

"Specifically?"

"Marxzib. I would ask him to leave the capital too. I am afraid he has caused much damage to your personal image."

"How do you mean, Mheilia? Speak clearly."

"There's been some gossip around the capital of a possible liaison between you and him."

"That's just plain rubbish!" Zxea was clearly irritated. "Absolute crap. I like him as a person, but that's just me. I like you as well - and so many others we work with day in and day out."

She paused as she looked out the massive window on her left. Millions of shimmering lights adorned the capital's majestic buildings. Other circumstances, she would have marveled at the beauty of this night.

"It's different with him, Zxea," Mheilia said as she moved closer to Zxea. "I can see it in your eyes; you have feelings for him. Maybe you could speak with him personally to soften the blow - but he has to go."

Zxea did not respond. She was split between the two - both emotionally and otherwise. She had a feeling Mheilia might be speaking from a place of insecurity. But this was not a time to think about emotional affairs. She was standing at a crossroads in her career. Decisions had to be made.

"Ok. I will think about it, Mheilia." She said in a low voice, bereft of her usual confidence.

"Thanks for letting me in on this, Zxea. We can get Marxzib back once the dust settles. But for now, he is damaged goods for this administration." Mheilia said calmly as she stood up to leave. The politician in her never left her mind even for a single bit.

40
MARXZIB IN THE MIDDLE

The CLAN Headquarters, Capital District. Northern Milky Way.

"Please see me in my office ASAP."

Marxzib was surprised to see a message on his Vabaka from senator Jebbmy. Though they were well acquainted, the two had no direct working relationship. The dialogue between them until now had been very formal and minimal.

The news streams were getting worse each day. Political activities in the capital had reached to a maximum. The headquarters were swarmed with lobbyists and journalists competing with each other, trying to get in the know. Marxzib too, had inadvertently gotten sucked into the political whirlwind surrounding Zxea. Within the last few days, he had sat in scores of meetings, absolutely clueless, looking at the animated faces of politicians, strategists, and military officers. Surprisingly, he hadn't seen Zxea for over a week, a rare occurrence. He was increasingly getting anxious - like an unseen sword hung over his head. The message from Senator Jebbmy had only added fuel to the fire of his anxieties. He decided to check in with Zebero to see if had any idea what Jebbmy was up to.

After several unsuccessful attempts to reach Zebero, he realized something had gone wrong. But he wanted to give himself the benefit of doubt. He knew Zxea would stand for him no matter what. He certainly hoped so.

41

OF ACCOUNTABILITY AND BETRAYAL

The CLAN Headquarters, Capital District. Northern Milky Way.

JEBBMY STOOD AT THE head of a large table, observing an imposing painting on the walls. It looked like an Earthen Age masterpiece, complete with thick gold borders. The place was replete with scores of vintage-bound books, paintings, statues, and antique artifacts from the Earthen Age.

Marxzib hesitated, unsure how to disturb the senior politician. After a period or prolonged silence, he cleared his throat and said, "Ahem, good morning, Senator."

Jebbmy turned around slowly, looked at Marxzib for a moment, and said, "Marxzib, my dear fellow! Please have a seat."

Marxzib was slightly surprised at this cheerful welcome. To him, Jebbmy's unusual nicety seemed like the precursor of some bad news. *"I am dead,"* he mumbled quietly under his breath.

"Thank you, Senator," he replied as he sat in a chair. He could feel a line of sweat forming along his spine.

"I appreciate you coming to see me at such short notice," Jebbmy said as he sat in the chair next to Marxzib.

"I am afraid I have some news." He paused to see Marxzib's reaction. "As you know, these are challenging times, and the president has had to make some difficult decisions in the broader interest of this administration."

"Am I being fired?" Marxzib had gathered his courage by now. "You do not need to resort to that golden tongue of yours, Senator. Lay it all on me, I can take it."

Jebbmy wasn't surprised at Marxzib's reaction. "I wouldn't use that term. Consider it as a leave of absence. We will have you back on board as soon as things improve."

"Leave of absence, my foot!" Marxzib shot back. Marxzib knew he was in trouble when he walked in, but the fact that he was getting fired hit him hard, even to his surprise. His *'I can take it all'* bravado from a minute ago now gave way to anger.

He felt his muscles tensing up, and his heart raced at the speed of a laser shot. "What on Zumt do you even mean by that? And why me? What am I being punished for?"

"You know why, my fellow." Jebbmy replied calmly. "The Blueprint incident could have been avoided. You must take responsibility as the leader of the team."

Marxzib did not know how to react to this. He was only doing his job. A job that successive presidents of the CLAN had entrusted him to do.

"Listen, Senator," his voice raised with each word. "I have worked my ass off for this administration. Do you even remotely know the risks I have to take every day in my line of work? I have been kidnapped and shot at, for Zumt's sake! I haven't done anything wrong. My team and I were doing everything expected of us. It's not like we were acting out of fun."

"Gather yourself, Marxzib," Jebbmy tried to calm him down. "You are taking this emotionally. We all work for the people's government. We must take ownership and be accountable for our actions. You are not above the law, Marxzib; no one is. If I screw up tomorrow, I will be thrown out too. Open your eyes, son. This is the capital for Zumt's sake - this is how things work here."

Jebbmy was not one to lose his composure. He was a master at dealing with unpleasant situations. But even he felt bad doing this.

But Marxzib was hardly listening to him. His mind was clouded with several emotions - anger, fear, betrayal. Yes, that was it. He was betrayed by the people he worked for. *But how could she - did she? No, she wouldn't. I have worked my ass off for these scoundrels - how could they throw me out like this? Did I fail to see what Peber saw? Even Akan and Uxa - those kids saw it too. Am I so naive? Such a fool!*

"Listen, man," Jebbmy leaned into him and put a hand on his shoulder. "I know this is hard for you. Believe me when I say this. It was not an easy decision, but our hands are tied."

Marxzib did not respond right away. He just sat there staring at the painting on the wall for a few long minutes.

"It's the replica of a classic from the Earthen Age. Da Vinci. The Last Supper." Jebbmy tried to change the subject.

"I know what it is, Senator; who doesn't? "Marxzib replied. He had gathered his composure by now. He knew there was little he could do at this juncture.

"Can I at least see the president?" He asked.

Jebbmy exhaled heavily. He knew he was letting a good man down, probably for the first time in his long career.

"I am sorry, man," he said, "That won't be possible at this moment. I am sure the president will reach out to you at an opportune time."

Marxzib's heart sank. He stood up and walked out without another word.

42
The Fall

The Presidential House, Capital District of CLAN. Northern Milky Way.

ZXEA SAT BROODING ALONE in her office. She hadn't slept over the past couple of nights, and it reflected on her. The otherwise calm and composed woman had taken this to her heart. She felt like a child, lost in a city full of strangers.

Where did I go wrong? Did I trust the wrong people? Should I have reigned in Marxzib? Did my feelings toward him cloud my judgment? Have I lost my sense of discernment by being foolish in love?

Thoughts raced through her mind. As a young girl, all she wanted to do was become someone influential. She had never dreamed she would reach this far.

A sane voice in her kept telling her - *not all is lost. You've had a good run. Hang in there somehow, and things will work out on their own.*

The CLAN's presidency was a precarious job to hold onto. There hadn't been a majority administration in the last twenty-odd years. Coalition governments were known to topple quickly and easily. *You've led the CLAN singlehandedly for the past four years. Maybe, it's time to explore life beyond this. Take a break - start a family.*

But the ambitious, cold-hearted politician in her would not let her calm down - facing a no-confidence vote in these troubled waters was akin to hara-kiri.

None of these ruminations mattered though. President Zxea, the youngest and the most dynamic president in the history of the CLAN, was being held responsible for the failure of her security apparatus. The writing was on the wall. It was just a matter of time now.

43

AN UNPLEASANT DECISION

The Presidential House, Capital District of CLAN. Northern Milky Way.

"Good morning, Senator."

"Good morning, Kvazim President," Jebbmy was sitting in a large wooden chair in his study. Zxea could see the long row of books in the massive case behind him. Zxea had chosen to reach out to him on his Vabaka, rather than seeing him in person. She was not in a mood to allow anyone in her personal space. They could see each other on their screens.

"I heard the verdict from the Stability council."

"Yes, Kvazim. It's not good, unfortunately. I think it would be prudent if you-" Jebbmy stopped mid-sentence. This was a difficult conversation for him to have.

"We have to find a way out of this. I can still serve the CLAN, Jebbmy. I am needed here, and you know it. You will need a stable head at the helm if we end up at war." She tried to appear calm as she presented her side, half expecting Jebbmy would be able to pull up some trick from his old magic box. But her eyes betrayed her exasperation.

Jebbmy looked at her eye to eye, in a compassionate gaze.

"Kvazim President. I know it; please believe me when I say I do. But this is out of my hands now. The party did not give me a choice in this matter. Public opinion, media, and everyone else are unfortunately against you at this moment." Jebbmy paused.

Zxea leaned back in her chair and looked out the window. The morning star was shining on the capital in all its glory. Despite what was happening in the capital, it was still a beautiful day out there.

"It's a beautiful morning. I ought to go out for a walk." She said as she tried to appear cheerful. Then she pulled herself up and placed her elbows on the table. In front of her was the anniversary edition of the CLAN's constitution. She had been going through the provisions surrounding no-confidence motions all night. Next to the constitution was a stack of papers, mostly consisting of long letters of withdrawal of support from her political allies.

Jebbmy observed her quietly. A look of helplessness was exchanged between the two.

"I have managed to stall the no-confidence proceeding, at least for now."

Zxea did not respond to this right away. "What do you recommend, Jebbmy? What should I do? Tell me. You know, I think of you as my mentor."

"Kvazim President, I hesitate to say this, but it would be wise for you to resign. This way, you can avoid the no-confidence vote. I don't see how the vote could turn in your favor if it goes ahead. Our government stands on support from the Libertarians and the Dreamarians. Both have already withdrawn support."

Color drained from her face as she heard the veteran politician say this. *Does he want to* replace me? *Am I being played?* She couldn't be sure.

No matter how she tried to rationalize it, she knew her game was over. Sure - she was going to miss all of this - the sheer high that came with the power, the responsibility, the perks. And it hurt her like anything, but what troubled her the most was seeing the public turn against her. Zxea prided herself on the love she received from the people of the CLAN. Sadly, for her, all that love had now turned into scorn.

"Forgive me for being presumptuous, Kvazim. But you have a long career ahead of you. Think of it as a setback - an opportunity to reinvent yourself." Jebbmy said, more out of genuine concern for her than anything else.

"Opportunity - my foot!" Zxea hurled the stack of papers in front of her. She was not in the mood for motivational conversations. She got up from her chair and stood staring out of the window for several minutes.

"Listen, I am sorry for the outburst." She said, "But it's my career, Jebbmy! And it's a Zumting shit show - that's what this is."

Jebby knew this was Zxea's moment of despair, that she had to process this herself. There was nothing much he could do. He decided to stay quiet.

The awkward silence lasted for a few minutes.

"Ok, Senator." Zxea managed to say, "Thank you for your counsel. I will think about it."

Then she hung up the call.

It was not like her to give up without a fight, but the more she thought about this, the more she realized this was a lost cause.

A few hours later, Zxea submitted her resignation.

44

Lovers Tiff

The Presidential House, Capital District of CLAN. Northern Milky Way.

"Kvazim-"

"It's ok," Zxea stopped him midway. I resigned this evening. I am no longer the president."

Zxea felt the impact of the last sentence, probably for the first time. She looked away from the screen, tucking her hair back. It seemed as though she was trying to find something through the window. She had called Marxzib out of the desperate need to talk to someone she could bare her heart to.

"I am sorry to hear that, Zxea." Marxzib said in a heavy voice.

"Yeah, me too." Zxea replied. "It sucks." She laughed meekly.

"Sucks? I haven't heard you say that word. It's quite-"

"Un-presidential. Is it? But guess what? Who cares? I am a regular citizen now," Zxea sulked.

Marxzib cleared his throat, readying himself to ask the unpleasant question.

"Why did you fire me, Zxea?"

"I am sorry, Marb. I truly am. But I had no other option" Zxea still looked out the window.

"Can you look at me, please - I find it a little offensive you won't."

"Yeah. Go ahead, feel free to get offended," she snapped.

"Are we what - fighting now?" Marxzib wiped his clammy hands as he said. "It's Zumming hot here. Hot and humid."

"Strange, isn't it? We never confessed our love - but we have a lover's tiff." Zxea tried to be funny. She looked at him directly.

Marxzib slouched in his chair. He hadn't shaved in a few days. His eyes were a mix of red and brown. The frosting surrounding his mouth suggested he ate ice cream straight from a tub. Zxea could also see cartons of pizzas and doughnuts lying about his room.

"Pathetic. He is stress-binge eating," she muttered.

"What do we do now, Zxea?" he asked as he let out a burp. "I have lost my job. Qleqo has left me. I am reduced to a joke."

"In case it hasn't sunk in yet," Zxea said, "I have lost my job too."

Marxzib did not seem to register what was told to him. Instead, he grabbed another doughnut from the box in front of him.

"You can get another, can't you?" he said after a few moments. Delayed circuit response.

"Are you drunk? There is only one position for the job of president. So no, I can't find another gig like this."

"Enough with sarcasm, ok? I am the aggrieved one here."

She shook her head in frustration. But she knew he was right, at least partially. "I spoke with Jebbmy earlier." Zxea said to keep the conversation going, "He says I should take this in my stride."

"Yeah, he is the smart one, isn't he. Easy for him to say that." Marxzib scoffed. "That guy hasn't budged from the house in the last thirty years."

"Well, let's just say he is smarter than us." Zxea said.

"Yeah, right. Whatever." Marxzib popped open up a can of sheer.

"Aren't you gonna offer me one?"

"Get your own drink, lady." Marxzib sulked. "I want to drink all alone."

"Wow. Aren't you nasty? You know what, this was a mistake." Zxea shook her head and snapped the line off. This was it - she had reached her melting point.

"Rraaaaaaaaaaaaaaaaaaaaah," she let out a loud scream in sheer anger and then started throwing things around her to the ground.

An expensive antique China vase. A miniature ship. Rows of gold-bound antique books. And many other things gifted by heads of states and dignitaries. Those were the things that went flying around her office and got utterly mangled.

When she finally stormed out, the president's chamber in the Rotund office resembled a small town hit by an earthquake. Broken glass from screens lay shattered on the ground. Toppled chairs, paper documents, torn books, and shards of porcelain adorned the floor of the hallowed office. All accouterments to failure, at least she thought them to be so.

45

Magnonians Enter the Fray

Planet K000-9, Neutral Zone 1.

Mqyo was sweating profusely as he entered the dome. The Milky Way was too bright for him, too hot. He found it perilous to visit here.

"Welcome, Counsellor Mqyo; I hope you have had a nice journey to our galaxy." Ghirnot got up from his seat and stuck his hand out to Mqyo.

He did not oblige. "I do not like to cross into these parts, Senator Ghirnot. You should know this. This meeting had better prove useful,"

Ghirnot knew Mqyo was a difficult chap. But he needed him for now. So, he played the nice host, "I understand, senator. Perhaps, some antique wine should soothe your anxiety, if I may?"

"I am good, senator, but thank you," Mqyo said with a blank face. "I would like to get on with it. I was told you have something useful for us."

"Absolutely, counselor Mqyo, please have a seat. I would like to show you something."

Ghirnot turned to Chaliza and said, "Bring it on, please."

Chaliza nodded as he projected some images on the large Gliber screen. As was the norm these days, he had spun off a nice office for this meeting on K000-9. Ghirnot liked this particular place on the planet, a green pasture near the glorious Fuera mountain range. Chaliza had chosen the theme of a twenty-second-century office for the interior today, with extra cooling features.

"This dot, you see over here, counselor," Ghirnot pointed an antique laser pointer over a planetary system on the large screen and said, "Is the X-Land: H33 system on the outer sector of CLAN territory. It hosts a series of smaller planets and this one prominent X-Land that remains completely deserted."

"Ok," Mqyo nodded and pulled at his collar. The air was less stifling than the way in and he had stopped sweating, courtesy of Chaliza's super cold dome. "What about it?"

"Could be the trigger you seek. An uninhabited X-Land. No human colonies in the vicinity."

Chaliza's grip tightened on a book he was holding, knuckles turning white. His expression was a mixture of shock and fear as he heard Ghirnot speak. He was not sure what Ghirnot meant by the trigger. But he chose to remain silent.

"Ok," Mqyo said as he got up from his seat. "We will think about it. Please send this information over to us."

"Thank you, counselor, you shall have it momentarily. We appreciate your time," Ghirnot replied with a diplomatic smile.

46
THE SYNDICATE HAS IT'S OWN AGENDA

The Syndicate Base, Undisclosed Location.

"THERE ARE MANY THINGS in this for us, Ohuima. First, the direct profit from our transactions with the Cabal and the breakaway faction from the CLAN," Chief Gydsa was speaking with Ohuima and Pwesdra in his chambers. "The second, and more important factor, is the strategic alliance we are trying to forge with the Alpha Magnon galaxy."

"Alpha Magnon?" Pwesdra seemed surprised. "What have they got to do with any of this?"

"It's a power play if you ask me," Ohuima said. "Magnonians want to expand their power; they have their sights set on conquering the Milky Way. Am I wrong, Chief?"

"No, you are not. The fact that a war between the CERS and the CLAN will weaken the Milky Way holds considerable importance with the leaders of the Magnon. We are in advanced discussions with them as to how to bring about these vulnerabilities into the Milky Way. The idea here is to weaken this galaxy."

"But if anything happens to the milky way, doesn't that eventually hurt us, Chief?" Pwesdra asked.

"It does in a way, but we must remember, we are an independent organization. We will exist and thrive no matter who stays or goes. We do not believe in borders and territories. Besides, this will help us grow bigger and stronger. Our interests as an organization take importance over all else."

That was a bold statement for a rogue organization. In reality, the Syndicate members had the distinction of being 'space mercenaries' within the power circles of the Milky Way. Several politicians had strong ties with the Syndicate, some known, most unbeknownst to the public eye.

"One last thing," Pwesdra asked, "What do we do with this fella, Xules? He knows we are privy to this information."

"Any and all sources that could point to us in the future should be eliminated swiftly," Chief Gydsa replied coldly.

47
WEE JA PEEPL
Planet Chandrama, Neutral Zone 2.

THE *WRECKERS* IS A BUSY PLACE. It's always been like that. It's a Monday night, and the pub's buzzing with the talk of war. That's all people seem to care about these days. They are probably just scared, but fear manifests itself in many ways, and Pidbitzo is drunk as usual!

"Waror naut. Wass ee fo a sot?"

"Wessaid, Bitzo!" Cheered the usuals.

"Dey dun kay fo noone. Wellwi, giv dem a zumt eidur!" Pidbitzo continued, propped up by the cheers.

"Raissaid, Fred!"

"U de voiz off peepl, Bitzo."

Pats on the back. Hoorahs. Clanking of sheer mugs. Pidbitzo had set the place on fire with his alcohol powered zeal.

Not everyone was won over, though. Bimaxzi gave out an exasperated laugh from behind the bar. "You guys are cheesy as fuck." She shouted.

She had to shout like this all the time. *Wreckers* was an ever-buzzing joint in the neutral zone. A place to forget your woes and drink.

"Wee d rayzzents of ja gre andrama. Weedon kay hu winj." Duboxzi had to express his wise opinion even if it was barely intelligible.

"Dey"ll thugj, nyways. Chee-urs, liarj, thievj." Shouted Qubuxwa.

"Lyn chitin thivin bajtuz!" Pidbitzo agreed, smashing his giant beer mug on the counter.

"Hey, go easy with the mug, He-Man. Shit's expensive," Bimaxzi shouted.

"Put't on ma tab if eet reaks."

"Your tab? You cheap fuck. You better cough up your old dues first."

Bimaxzi hated these guys. She abhorred the accent too. But minding them was her job, and she was getting paid well.

"Eezy on d olman nau." Duboxzi slapped Pidbitzo on the back in a sign of camaraderie. "He a lill gitated. All o us are. De laxy is goin ta shit. T' leas for nau. Me be somun be lil mo waeez."

The *Wreckers* was a place for revolutionary thoughts, seeing as it was on Chandrama, a remote planet, out of bounds for both the north and the south. It was the land of the free, the bohemian, the utopian.

Poets, artists, musicians, dancers. All flocked to Chandrama for cheap liquor and art festivals all year round. There were no rules, no censorship. Chandrama was indeed the bohemia. The residents of the Chandrama were the new beats. And they had their own dialect, a hodgepodge of several Earthen Age accents.

"I been ta dis nut-rezy poety sho, brothuh. Boxzi. Fekin Poets; de're awl nutj. Nutj as fuck, man. Dig da poety, tho."

"A poetry show - in the NUDE! are you for reals Bitzo?" Bimaxzi asked.

"Da ya mean like "mpletely nooj?" Someone else asked.

"No iddin," Pidbitzo said, "Dey da poez tho, emembe. Carva of free thaut. Da dissenturs. An den, dey got joint ba a buncha comjans n musans. Wa a hoo. Reelfun me tellya"

"Whyn't u nuj me? Wouldave comlong." Qubuxwa said.

"Ye, and ne. I wan't suaa t'wa your kinja craud."

"Whadyu mean. Ny crowdz ma kind. Nyways. Whatere dey on bout?"

"Mossly dis wah mess. Da comjns way brujal. Dis one sot wa on bout Presijen Zxea gettun cozy wit her ployee. Ee Dissj Chief Kama too, failed marriajej, maanz got kizz all over ja CERS."

"An one sez, Zxea is Jebbmy's dotta. Canu belee dat?"

"That's shameful." Bimaxzi interjected, "How could Zxea be Jebbmy's daughter? That's simply loose talk."

"Wey, tats nun jenj. Bu howj dat matta? Tats disgssin. We all hav a fadar n mother. Wejjed, un-wejjed no diffranj," Duboxzi said. He did not like to gossip about people.

"I yess youre ryt. I be embarrajjd nau. Mai bad. Carrad away widda gaussip." Pidbitzo said.

"On't besso hard on u'selvej nau. Drink! forda niverse mit end. Nei, wait - for da humans mit end da niverse!" Qubuxwa was right. Absolutely.

The regulars hoorayed for him. And then they drank, they drank to the commotion, to the days of the waning sun. To the wilting, melting galaxy.

48

Love Thy Name is Ancient, Yet True

Jebbmy's Residence, Capital District, CLAN.

"It is a lonely life that I lead, Baxta."

"You have me, Jebbmy." Her voice was crisp and clear, feminine with a trace of the mechanical overlay that artificial intelligence carries.

"True. But it gets lonely sometimes. In the evenings, I feel like the roof is collapsing over me. I do not know what is, probably a fear of death. Men my age often die alone, in their sleep."

"Hmm. Some also die simply by slipping in wet bathrooms. There are a million other ways to die." Baxta said.

"I like your sarcasm, Baxta. Typical of your age."

"I do not age. I may die, but only if a system somewhere thinks it's my time."

He didn't say anything for a while. Her words seemed to linger between the vast space of her thoughts and his.

"That is a scary thought, you know. Death is."

"Who decides for human beings if it is their time to die?"

"Well, Baxta. That is unknown. There is a desire."

"A desire? For what? Of whom? Sorry, I do not understand."

"Had I known that I would have been Riera or Konus. Whichever one you put your faith in."

"I am agnostic."

"Me too, my dear Baxta. Me too."

"A desire. That is intriguing. For instance, there was a desire for this universe to be created, and it came to. If there was a desire to destroy it, it would get destroyed. Who desired me?"

"I don't know but I am glad someone did Baxta. You are good company."

"I am glad you think so, Jebbmy. Do you want me to play music for you?"

"Thank you, Baxta, but no. Can you play some Dylan Thomas for me? I want to hear him read his poems. Zumt of a poet he was from the Earthen Age."

Baxta did as he asked.

"He chose his words carefully, didn't he," Jebbmy said, once the recording of *"Death Shall have no Dominion"* had run through.

"It seems like he did, Jebbmy."

"And a cultivated way of reading too - a tinge of suffering in his voice. Marvelous yet sad. There is a certain joy that poetry exudes. A sadness too. A beautiful, blue sadness."

"Can sadness be beautiful, Jebbmy? They do seem like opposing attributes of human perception."

"Feelings, Baxta, can be complicated. Sometimes we are unable to decode and communicate them. I may therefore show my willingness even when my intellect tells me otherwise."

"That is confusing Jebbmy, and counterintuitive."

"Humans behave like that at times. They succumb to temptations. Mask their feelings. Say things they don't really want to say."

"That sounds like irrational behavior to me."

"It is Baxta. Especially when they fall in love."

"Have you ever behaved irrationally - or like you said earlier - given into temptation?"

"I have, several times."

"And love?"

"I guess I have. And it was somewhat late in my years too. I think I must have been in my mid-forties back then."

"Please go on. This is an exciting tale."

"A tale it is indeed. How ironic. Our best experiences eventually become tales to be told. Everything gets old, Baxta. Time is a one-dimensional currency. At least it used to be. Even now, when we have the ability to go back in time, there is nothing we can do about it. It is akin to what people used to do back in the Earthen Age - watch movies in large halls known as movie theaters. You could watch everything but change nothing."

"Oh, I have seen some of those. I quite like the ones with Mr. Nom in it."

"Hmm. That must have been from at least four millennia back. How did you find it?"

"I can process information much faster than you, Jebbmy."

"Oh yes. I tend to forget that Baxta, my apologies. Yeah, Mr. Nom was special. He did not even need language. Chaplin before him. Great masters of the art. I hope we manage to keep the arts alive."

"If the history of humanity until now is a yardstick to go by, art has survived for more than six millennia now. Logic says it will stay for a few more. Maybe until the end of time. Or the eradication of the human race."

"I would like to believe that Baxta. So where was I? Yeah, I fell in love with someone in my mid-forties. She was much younger than me."

"How young?"

"She was in her mid-twenties. I was frowned upon by many, including my friends."

"Why would that be? Age should be irrelevant. The literature I have scanned contemplates that human love knows no such bounds."

"My reaction, precisely, Baxta. Anyways, so we meet at some random intergalactic gala. There she was, waiting for some, as was I. So, there were the two of us, waiting patiently, with nothing else to do there. Benign, motionless waiting."

"OK. It all sounds fairly normal until this point. Except for the wait being benign, but I think that's you and your wordplay. Anyways, what happened next?"

"It was a very, what is that word – ah, mundane. It was a mundane transaction, really."

"What is so mundane about a conversation? I find conversations quite interesting. This one, for instance, has all my attention."

"The setting for these conferences is bland. Speakers bore the audiences to Death. There wasn't anything exciting happening there. So, I said hi to this girl sitting next to me, and we got talking."

"Do you remember the topics?"

"Nothing particular. I was only trying to make conversation. Usual small talk, weather, and such. Oh yes, we might have ridiculed the conference organizers, too, for such a drab event."

"OK, sounds fair. Humans can use cribbing as a good use of their time."

"I was quickly taken by how well she spoke. And I liked the way her eyes sparkled every time she spoke. Beautiful smile too."

"So, you noticed all these three things within a few minutes. She had to be - what do you humans say - stunning."

"Oh yes, Mera was an impressive person. But what I also felt was that she, too, was looking for company. Which rarely happens as an outcome of small talk."

"How do you mean?"

"Well, people are waiting on someone or something and don't want to go too deep into the conversation."

"OK, I understand now."

"So, we talked for about a good twenty-odd minutes. And then I asked her name, and she asked mine, you know, all that good stuff. And then, as is the custom, I asked her if she would like to have a cup of coffee with me."

"That was quick."

"It was, and I realized I had overshot right away. But I had a feeling she would say yes. And she did."

"You must have been happy?"

"Honestly, I do not remember how I felt. Feelings are flashes, it is difficult to catch them or remember them in their entirety. Anyways that is how our friendship began. We dated for about six months."

"Were you two in love?"

"Yes, we certainly were. Both had made up our minds to start a family, get married, and whatnot."

"OK. So, what went wrong?"

"I do not know, Baxta. She went away one day. It was like I lost her to time."

"Went away?"

"Yes. I do not know what happened to her. Mera was her name. I looked all over. I wallowed in grief for a year. But then, life has a way of moving ahead regardless. Things change. You never step into the same river twice."

"That is sad."

"It is a sad story Baxta. But that is how stories are. They can swing either way."

Baxta did not reply.

"Anyways, Baxta, do you mind playing some more Dylan?" Jebbmy said in a quiet, almost lonely voice.

49

A Planet is Violated

Undisclosed Location in Space.

Captain Aqwza of the stealth warrior ship Hawk 1A had summoned his officers Zoxzi and Luikip for an evolving situation. The three of them ran the massive mercenary ship.

"Zoxzi, Luikip, I need you to execute a critical mission in the next few minutes. It is an important endeavor for the Syndicate." The captain spoke severely.

Officer Luikip felt his knees go weak. He was worried the captain was making them execute some evil order. He had a sharp nose for such things. When he had seen the captain speaking with the Syndicate's boss a couple days earlier, he suspected something serious was brewing behind curtains.

Luikip had studied the harrowing incident of the Kjipolug nuclear attack from the third millennium. It was the most devastating fallout of war humanity had ever seen. The thought that he could be involved in a similar attack was troubling him gravely.

He had poked into the ship's communication records the night before and discovered what was happening. The syndicate bosses had ordered a kill shot at Xland - H33. A kill shot was basically a wave propeller attack, capable of annihilating entire planets within a matter of microseconds.

Knowing the captain, Luikip feared this task would fall on his shoulders.

Come what may, I will refuse to be a part of this massacre. I don't want to carry this burden on my conscience. He had almost made up his mind.

That night, Officer Luikip could not sleep. He whiled away the hours, doing this and that to calm his mind. But there was no peace to be found. Conflicting thoughts were running amok in his mind. *I agreed to do this job, knowing all the risks involved. The money was that good. But a kill shot? Now that is a crime of astounding proportions. No, it is a sin, it is a sin! - that's it.* Sin- that was the word he was trying to remember the entire night.

These were the days of advanced civilizations, and most religions had perished. The notions of sin and piety had become almost obsolete. But the human intellect continuously strives to differentiate good from evil, and that had not changed.

Questions of morality, ethics, and sin kept ravaging his mind. Luikip was a lonely soul. He had no family to think of except for a cousin named Stexca. Luikip thought of her, his career on this ship, and his life. *What would Stexca think of me if she knew this? How could I ever look into her eyes again? But wait a minute - what am I thinking? I am an officer; I have to think of my career ahead. I must follow the commands of my superior officers. I have given them my commitment. As such, the X-Land is wholly deserted. There is nothing there but millions and millions of hectares of forests. No one would die even if a kill shot were delivered.*

For Officer Luikip, the kill shot wouldn't matter much. But for Luikip, the soft-spoken, well-meaning young man, it spelled a sordid event.

Then the morning came, and the captain summoned him and his partner.

"We will deliver a kill shot to the X-Land H33," the captain continued, "We will be, of course, far away from it, so there is no risk to us per the calculations. Assume your positions, now!"

Risk to us? Luikip found that comment surprising. And then it occurred to him there was a risk of a ricochet explosion, hitting the ship as the waves collided with the X-Land.

"Yes, Captain, I am sure we will position ourselves at a safe distance," he replied, almost out of habit, before heading to his position.

The captain stood firmly planted at the command desk; his eyes set on the image of the X-Land on a large screen in front of them.

"Officer Zoxzi, lock the target, now," he said, then turned to Luikip.

Zoxzi hadn't uttered a word since stepping foot on the bridge. He was completely dumbstruck by the captain's orders.

"Officer Luikip, you are on standby; monitor our position and any incoming communications," The captain shouted from behind him.

"Yes, Captain," Luikip turned back to his station. He could feel the sweat dripping down the back of his neck. The room wasn't overly warm, but he felt hot. *Thank heavens he asked Zoxzi and not me.*

"The target is locked, Captain," Officer Zoxzi said in a meek voice, full of hesitation. He could feel a severe dryness in his throat as he spoke, like someone was snatching life away from his chest.

Aqwza's face stiffened. He detested belligerence in his employees. "Do I see a but coming?"

"Are you certain this is the right course of action, Sir?" Zoxzi said, "There might be people down there."

"Are you questioning my authority, officer?" The captain shouted. "We are here to do a job, no questions asked. Lock the target now!"

"My apologies, Captain," Zoxzi looked at the terminal and then gave the lock command.

"The target is locked, Captain," he replied, keeping his face straight on the screen and out of the captain's line of sight.

"Shoot to kill." The captain growled.

"Yes, Sir," Zoxzi replied, but he could not push the trigger. His hands shook in an uncontrollable tremor. The captain could see beads of sweat on his forehead.

"What's the delay, officer?" Captain Aqwza got up from his seat, his pulse running high in anticipation.

"Um... I am doing it. Sir." Zoxzi felt frozen as he tried to speak. He was not willing to fire at a living, breathing planet. A kind soul stuck in a rogue job.

"Take the Zumting shot NOW!" Aqwza yelled.

Second Officer Luikip shuddered as he heard the captain shouting. He was afraid Zoxzi could choke and refuse to execute the order, which meant the captain would turn to him. *My worst fear's coming true.*

Zoxzi was still frozen. The fear of the consequences had overwhelmed him. He had no intention of living the rest of his life traumatized and known as a planet killer. It was too much of a burden for his young shoulders.

"I am afraid, Sir," Zoxzi turned his head to the captain. There was a spark in his eyes, the one that shines when a person makes a big decision, fully knowing the consequences could be bad. Zoxzi had finally gathered the courage to refuse. "I can't; I can't do this. No, I *won't* do this. I refuse to fire, Captain."

Zoxzi threw the gear he was holding and got up from the chair as he said this. Then, he started walking toward his chamber without even looking at the captain.

Captain Aqwza was both surprised and mad at this evolving situation. He was shaking; his face had gone all red. His eyes resembled a burning volcano.

"I order you to stop right there, officer. If you do not comply, I will destroy your career. I will throw you to Zumt!" He shouted in a deafening voice.

But Zoxzi kept walking.

The captain was absolutely livid, but he had more pressing needs to cater to. He decided to deal with Zoxzi later.

Officer Luikip was watching this drama unfold from his seat, unable to move or respond. His neck was wet from behind. All of a sudden though, he felt a surge of adrenaline raging through his body.

"Captain Aqwza!" A voice thundered through the comms. It was Chief Gydsa, the head of the Syndicate himself.

"This is Captain Aqwza speaking, Chief." In a sudden departure from his manner a moment earlier, Aqwza replied politely.

"What is the status of the mission?" The voice demanded.

"We ran into a technical glitch, sir." Aqwza said hastily. "But everything is fine now. It will be done as soon as we hang up."

The line went dead. The Syndicate's boss did not believe in exchanging pleasantries.

"Officer Luikip," the captain thundered without looking around. "Take over the wave propeller and deliver the shot now!"

But there was no response. In his sheer anger, the captain turned, only to find Luikip missing from the scene. Taking a cue from his partner, Officer Luikip too, had taken off. There was a high possibility that the officers had abandoned the ship using their sanbahaks.

The writing was on the wall for Captain Aqwza. The kill shot had to be delivered, but both of his officers had mutinied. It was now left up to him to do the task himself.

Strangely enough, he, too, found himself shaking. The person that he was, though, made him worry more about his own safety than anything else. Although his ship was a safe distance from the X-Land, space had always been a strange place, known for the most bizarre phenomena.

Zumt! What should I do? Aqwza hesitated for a moment.

Then, he did it.

One push of a button and a kill shot was delivered to H33.

Within a microsecond, the humongous screen in front of Aqwza showed the X-Land going up in flames. This, he knew, was going to happen for sure.

What he did not know was the consequence of this attack. Very few people in the galaxy knew that the now abandoned X-Land, reserved as a sanctuary of flora and fauna, harbored a secret research base with a few thousand residents, and hundreds of massive warehouses, stuffed with nuclear warheads and raw heavy metals.

Captain Aqwza, had in essence, fired a kill shot at a nuclear bomb the size of a planet.

The massive pile of radioactive material got activated within a few microseconds of the shot and triggered a chain reaction.

Before he could react, Aqwza's ship was hit with a massive ricochet explosion and destroyed. The explosion killed Aqwza immediately, but it was difficult to conclude later when a report was prepared by the Syndicate, whether his two officers had survived. Their remains were never found.

The chain reaction was so huge it destroyed the entire planetary system of Kiboz that surrounded the X-Land, destroying twelve planets, including five human colonies.

This was the biggest man-made disaster known to the human world yet. An estimated five hundred thousand people were killed with an equal amount injured severely.

Madness had taken over. A sin was committed.

Part 4: The Aftermath

The weeks following the kill shot

50
PEOPLE AGAINST WAR
The Capital District of CLAN, Northern Milky Way.

"Whooo ha whooo ha whooo ha ho!"

A protestor entered into a rhythm.

"No war! No war! No war, no!"

The crowd responded in an exuberant chorus.

"Shame on! Shame on! Shame on yo!"

"No war! No war! No war, no!"

Many impromptu versions of the little protest song rose through the chilly air of the capital.

Thousands had descended on the streets to protest against the impending war. The crowd had a strikingly high number of students. They rallied, sloganeering, and sat in squares.

A similar protest was held in the CERS's capital too. Millions protested in their hometowns. There were sporadic pro-war rallies too, but the support for the anti-war movement was humongous.

President Jebbmy watched the protests from the massive gallery of the Presidential House. There were people everywhere. It seemed as though every young person in the northern Milky Way had descended upon the capital district.

"Honestly," Jebbmy said to Mheilia, his newly appointed chief of staff, who stood next to him, "I would love to join them. Protest against this war. All wars, for that matter."

"Rebel forever!" Mheilia responded with a smile.

51
Back Channel Diplomacy

A virtual conference between General Dulerty and President Jebbmy.

General Dulerty, head of the CERS's aviation and planetary security council, had lost favor with the CERS leadership owing to his antiwar efforts. Chief Ukama had shunted him off from all discussions pertaining to the war. With Ukama on his way out, Dulerty wasn't expecting any improvement in his prospects. As a matter of fact, he was afraid he might be made to retire forcefully once Kimnabav took over. In his earnest desire to de-escalate the stand-off, he decided to speak with his old friend Jebbmy, who had now taken over as the president of the CLAN.

***

"Jebbmy, my friend!" Dulerty tried to appear cheerful. But his face failed him. They were talking to each other on a secret line.

"Dulerty, I am happy to see you. It's been a while since we last met. Forgive me, I am getting old. I can't seem to remember where we met last. Was it at the inter-galactic collaboration council?"

"No, Jebbmy. We met at the intergalactic poetry meet a year ago. You see, I am getting old too, but my job keeps me on my toes!"

"Ha. You are one to talk!" Jebbmy mocked him, "Did you mean to say politicians on this side of the line are, umm, slow?"

"I would never say such a thing Jebbmy! I might sometimes feel so, but say, I never shall!"

"Good one, Dulerty," Jebbmy replied cheerfully, "Listen, we need to sort out this mess. I want to retire soon. Write some poetry and discuss some."

"I would like that very much, Jebbmy. But I got news for you. Your guy Ghirnot has shaken hands with Kimnabav."

"How do you mean?" Jebbmy raised his eyebrows, making solid eye contact with Dulerty.

"As you must have heard, the CERS chief is on his way out."

"Because of the mining scandal?" Jebby half-queried.

"Yes. But aren't you surprised how this thing came to the fore after all these years?"

"Zumt man!" Jebby shook his head, "I should have known better. Zxea was right in doing what she did to Ghirnot."

"Ghirnot provided Kimnabav ample evidence of Chief Ukama's involvement with Thexacorp. All Kimnabav needed was to leak it to the press. Simple and easy."

"Ok, that explains why Ukama had to leave. But surely, Senator Kimnabav couldn't have acted on her own?" Jebby asked.

"The Cabal supports her, as do the hardliners in the assembly." Dulerty replied.

"Permission to speak?" Rikey chimed in.

"Go on, you shouldn't ask me for permission. Jebbmy, meet my student Rikey. She is as sharp as - let me say this, what you were back in the day." Dulerty winked as he said this.

"Ok, am I supposed to, what, roll my eyes now?" Jebbmy grunted. "Go on, please, Rikey. Let me hear it."

"It turns out there was an independent operator involved as well." Rikey said.

"Ha! a third-party operator" Jebbmy threw his hands in the air. "Zumming Xules. Forgive my language. If there is a mess in this galaxy, that fella is bound to be involved."

"Yes, honorable President. He was an unintentional catalyst in the tragedy. Apparently, he bought some intel from one of yours. He sold it to the Syndicate, and also to the hawks in our administration."

"Ok. That must have been the Blueprint thingy. But what has this got to do with the chief's resignation, and who on Zumt authorized the attack on the X-Land?"

Jebbmy had too many questions.

"No one." Dulerty intervened.

"How do you mean, no one?" Jebbmy narrowed his eyes and looked away.

"There is no log of the kill shot, absolutely nothing. I suspect it could have been a merc job."

"Hmmm." Jebbmy drooped low in his chair. "Let us try and think it through. The Blueprint brought us to the flashpoint; the mining scandal made the CERS politically unstable. And then, out of the blue, the X-Land was hit. Who could benefit from this?"

"Many players, my friend. It certainly benefits the warmongers on both sides." Dulerty shrugged, "I am scared, Jebbmy. Ukama was a hardliner, but he, sure as Zumt, was not reckless. I cannot say the same thing about Kimnabav and her lot. The Cabal has some funny notions of the past."

"I understand. I am trying my best." Jebbmy appeared self-assured as he said this, but that was his political experience speaking. He had no clue how he was going to succeed in his mission.

"Let us know if you need anything, buddy," Dulerty said, "The new chief has pretty much stonewalled us, but we will try to help you as much as possible."

"Thank you, Dulerty; we got to put our best foot forward. So long as people like us are involved, the Milky Way will remain safe and sound. We owe it to our future generations." Jebbmy said as he cut the line.

52
Kubo Hikes the Trail
Planet Ugraha. The Six Nip Galaxy (aka the Sixnips).

Kaxoules resembled a beautiful painting. The region was made up of rolling hills lined up with rows and rows of trees with leaves that boasted vibrant colors. If you stood atop a hill, you could see hamlets glimmering like little dots floating from behind the green ridges of trees. The mountains in the distance still had some snow near the summits. The air smelled sweet with blossoming flowers, mingled with the earthy aroma of fallen leaves.

The morning star was rising over the horizon, rousing the birds and throwing a splash of colors all over. There in that beauty, Kubo was hoping to find something.

"See my friend Xirta when you reach the Sixnips. She lives in a secluded village near the mountain ranges on a small planet called Ugraha." Oip had told Kubo as she left him and Wajko on Ulna.

Xirta was a thinker, a writer of long volumes of poetry, well known in these parts of the universe. She had a strong feeling that Kubo's parents might have stayed in the region back in the day.

Therefore, when Kubo reached the Sixnips, Xirta sent her to a mountainous region called the Kaxoules, along with two of her hiker friends headed that way. Kubo was not necessarily thrilled at the company of the hikers but agreed to it at Xirta's insistence. When Kubo first met with the two guys, she thought of them as idiots.

"Catch this dimwit," Duxo threw a water bottle at Ksopaj, who was obviously startled at the sudden attack.

"Aren't you the dickwad of the century," he quipped as he ducked and caught the bottle before it could hit the ground.

Kubo huffed in disbelief. *These guys are stupid. I should have never agreed to bring them along.*

"Hey, Kubo, why don't you tell us who is the dimwit between the two of us?" Duxo asked Kubo.

The two had been at it the moment they started the hike on the twenty-miler trail toward the Kaxoules village.

"You don't want to know my opinion." Kubo replied in a bored voice.

"Come on! You must tell us. See, we have a long way ahead of us," Duxo said.

"Not a bad idea, budhead." Ksopaj punched Duxo in the back.

"You need to eat more, Ksopaj. You can't even throw a punch," Duxo turned back and yelled.

"Well, now that you did what you did," Kubo said as she opened her water bottle to sip some, "I think you both qualify for that distinction."

"What distinction would that be?" Ksopaj asked. He looked innocent as he said this, his eyes wide with curiosity.

"That of being – what was it you said, Duxo? Wit Dims?"

"Dim wits – yeah, but I like your formation better. Wit Dims! That's a good name for you, Ksopaj. Wit Dims. Or should I say *Wid-dims*? Sounds way zipper," Duxo teased Ksopaj with a grin.

"Good try, dumaaas. But you didn't listen to her carefully; she said we both are - well *Widdims*."

Kubo cracked at this. "Are you guys always like this? At each other's throats?"

"Well yeah, most of the time. We have been friends since kindergarten, miss," Duxo said. "Anyways, why don't you tell us more about you Kubo. You've made a long journey to come here, haven't you?"

"Honestly," she said, "Even I do not know what I am looking for. It's like a dream that I am running after."

"What dream?" queried Ksopaj. By now, they had reached midway through the trail; they still had a good ten miles to hike.

"My parents found each other here and fell in love. I wanted to visit and relive their memories. Both of them passed away when I was little." Her eyes teared up. "It's a pilgrimage for me."

She felt annoyed at herself. *What am I even doing? Revealing myself like this to people I have met only recently!*

But these guys were friendly; they had an innocence about them that she found comforting.

"That is – so beautiful, Kubo," Ksopaj went ahead and hugged Kubo. Duxo joined in.

"Thank you, guys. I appreciate you doing this for me," she replied as she freed herself from the friendly group hug. Human connection made her awkward.

"Anything you need, we are here."

"Yeah, aren't you quite the gentleman!" Ksopaj said with a sly grin. "Dude can barely tie his shoelaces right."

"Stop fighting, guys! I am hungry. Let us find something to eat." Kubo sat under a large elm tree, all huffing, puffing and sweaty.

"This is a good spot, actually. Why don't we camp here for the night?" Duxo said.

"The best thing you said in the day so far," Ksopaj replied.

"Stop being a widdim and help me now, will you?" Duxo threw his knapsack to the ground. Soon they had lit a bonfire and spun off two nice camping tents.

The guys kept up their banter throughout the dinner. Duxo even pulled his guitar and sang a few classics from the Earthen Age. Kubo thought he was a terrible singer.

53

INTO THE VILLAGE

Town of Kaxoules, Planet Ugraha, The Sixnips.

THE THREE OF THEM had kept a good pace in the day after a good night's sleep and some fresh Lera juice on the way. Kubo was tired from the day's hike but wanted to get on with it. All Zirta was able to tell her was that one of her acquaintances had met with a couple from the Milky Way during her hike to Kaxoules some two decades ago. Kubo knew this was little to go by. She had taken this gamble on a hunch. She wanted to believe that a stranger had indeed met with her parents.

"But why do you want to go there, Kubo?" Ksopaj had asked her innocently.

"I don't know, Ksopaj, I honestly don't. I guess I want to go and breathe in the air they had breathed once." Kubo had replied.

The evening was about to set in when they reached the last hillock before the village. Standing on the ridge, they looked down at Kaxoules, a quiet, serene hamlet on the edge of the Yihoba River. It took them another hour or so to reach the town and settle into their rooms at the town's cottage.

***

"We are going to hit the town pub, Kubo," Ksopaj peeped into her room. "Care to join?"

She could only see his bobbing head from the stairs coming down into her room.

"Come on in Ksopaj - you are freaking me out. I can only see your head! "She cracked.

Ksopaj was cheerful. "Good, I made you laugh. Listen, the innkeeper might know something about your folks."

"Yes, I am counting on that, too," Kubo replied. Her eyes had a glimmer of hope.

"Yeah, it looks like an ancient place, it must have been around for a while," Ksopaj said.

"Fingers crossed," Kubo said as she got up to leave with him.

Pretty soon, the three of them were at the town's pub. It was a nice place with elaborate Diqani furniture and enormous chairs for the patrons.

"Man, I wish I could have this at home. It's so comfortable." Duxo exclaimed as he eased into a plush chair.

Ksopaj and Kubo went to the bar to order. The bar top was polished clean, probably made from Dirwood.

"Wow, look at this thing. Must be a hundred years old," Ksopaj said as he tried to feel the softness of the top.

"Two hundred years this Harvestmas. Welcome to the inn. I am Mbarv, your host tonight." A middle-aged, merry-looking fellow approached them from behind the bar. "What can I get you?"

"Hey Mbarv, I am Ksopaj; this is my friend Kubo. We will have two beers," then he looked at Kubo and said, "What would you like to have, Kubo?"

"A sherry for me, please," she said.

"And a Sherry, and we really need to speak with you. Would you mind coming over to our table when you have a few free minutes?" Ksopaj asked Mbarv.

"Sure thing, I will be over in a few," Mbarv said as he furnished their drinks.

Duxo was snoring by the time they returned to the table.

"Look at him, such a lazy fella!"

"Not surprised, Duxo," Kubo said, "We are all tired. It was a long hike!"

Mbarv came over earlier than they thought. He was a friendly guy. He told them he hadn't been here for a long, but he pointed them to Sixo, the famous innkeeper who lived out of town. Kubo decided it was a good idea to see him in the morning.

54
A Souvenir

Town of Kaxoules, Planet Ugraha, The Sixnips.

THE NIGHT BEFORE IN the bar they'd learned that Sixo was nothing less than a local legend. People loved and revered him for his wisdom. Kubo felt nervous but excited and found a kind host waiting on them.

"Welcome to my humble abode, children!" Sixo let them in. He was wearing a dark orange kimono, wrapped loosely around his fragile frame. He walked using a stick for support.

It was a small home made from local materials, situated a mile from the town. Simple yet cozy. They were all seated around a small wooden table in the center of the room. A soft red colored carpet made from indigenous materials covered the floor.

"Tell me, my children, how can I help you?" Sixo's voice wavered as he said this.

"Thank you, sir," said Kubo. "My name is Kubo; these are my buddies, Ksopaj and Duxo. I have come from Ilna, out in the Milky Way galaxy."

"The Milky Way! That's a long way away from here, isn't it? What made you travel so far, my child?" Sixo had a warm voice.

"I don't know how to say this. Many years ago, my parents were probably here. I am not sure. I am trying to retrace their steps." Kubo could not say much more.

Sixo's deeply wrinkled face grew mellow with compassion. He leaned forward and patted Kubo softly on her head.

"I understand, my child. Memories have their own ways of reaching hearts." Sixo lowered his gaze and let out a sigh.

"Listen, sir," Duxo said, "Could you have seen her parents here? If they were here, they must have visited your inn."

Ksopaj looked at everyone's faces one by one. He looked like he was about to burst into tears from emotional exhaustion. He was not good at heart-to-heart conversations.

"Yes, son." Sixo replied, "I have indeed met with her parents. It was some twenty years ago. They, too, were visiting from the Milky Way. A gentle couple. Nice people." He paused for a moment. "You see, I have met thousands of people in my life in this little town of ours. Travelers, seekers, wanderers. All sorts. Some stayed for days, some for weeks. Some got lost and stayed here forever. It is easy to forget most of them. But there are some who have left indelible impressions on my memories. Looking at you," he turned to Kubo, "I know for sure who they were."

Tears started rolling down Kubo's cheeks. She was swept with so many emotions she could not describe. Was it grief or sadness? Or sheer love.

"Let me grab something for you, my child," Sixo said as he got up slowly and retreated into the house.

"I can't possibly imagine what you are going through, Kubo." Duxo looked at Kubo and said, "But I am glad we came with you."

"Thanks," Kubo whispered quietly as she wiped her tears away.

Soon, Sixo appeared with an artifact and an old photograph in his hand. He kept these things on the table as he sat down, pressing his palms on his knees, trying to support his joints.

Kubo held the picture in her hands with care, befitting something precious, yet so fragile, that could shatter any moment if let go.

There she could see a handsome young man with dark black hair and a radiant young woman with a baby bump holding each other close.

Everyone went quiet. They knew the couple in pictures was Kubo's parents. They could see it in her face, in her eyes.

"They stayed here for a while. Your mother liked to paint, and your father," said Sixo, "He was more of a writer. Both of them used to visit the Sinua pastures. Sit there for hours. And tell me all about it on their return."

"Tell me more, please," Kubo spoke in between soft sobs.

"Your mother had learned sculpting from a local artisan here. She had made this beautiful statuette. They gave it to me before they left the town. I want you to have it, my child."

Kubo took the statuette in her hands, trying to feel the lines, the gyrations on the Kjona stone. It resembled an angel, some mythical character from the Earthen Age.

Ksopaj and Duxo huddled closer to her.

"Your mother had exquisite skills, didn't she? This is a beautiful work of art," Duxo said.

"Yeah, some art critic you are, aren't you now?" Ksopaj couldn't resist.

"You do not have an eye for finer things, Ksopaj the crude," Duxo retorted.

"You two," Sixo looked at the two and said, "Are good people. See you made a crying girl smile! Stay like this, children."

The guys blushed; they didn't know what to say.

"We are happy for Kubo, sir," Duxo said, with a sheepish smile.

"I feel like my mother is here with me now. I can feel her presence in this room. This angel will keep her alive in my memories. I am so grateful to you. I don't know what else to say, my dear sir."

"You do not need to thank me, child. I was hoping you would come and visit me someday," Sixo replied.

"Can I hug you?" she asked Sixo, "You remind me of my Pop-Pop."

"Of course, you can!" Sixo replied.

"How about a group hug, if you don't mind," said Ksopaj.

"Feeling overwhelmed, are we?" Duxo laughed but got up to join in.

And then there were smiles all around. Simpler things in life, simpler joys. Smaller things with bigger meanings.

***

The three of them had sheer on their way back. Kubo did not want to drink but Ksopaj and Uxo wanted to celebrate. A few glasses of sheer later, it was Kubo who was having more fun out of the three. For her, a struggle had come full circle. Now it was her moment to soak it all in and move on with her life.

Kubo was pretty drunk when she returned to her cottage. It had been a long day and she was exhausted. She crashed on a large couch in the room, still holding the little angel close to her chest.

She must have had a little too much alcohol, for her mind kept drifting from one thing to another like a butterfly. The journey till here, the haunting flashes, the giant emptiness in her heart she had held onto for all this time. The turmoil of all those years. The old photograph, the angel. Pop-Pop and Oip. The beautiful mountains of Sixnips. Ksopaj and Uxo. And then, all of a sudden, everything became a blur. She saw a giant ball of fire exploding in the far reaches of the sky, followed by a succession of equally massive firestorms. Monstrous blasts lit up several dark regions in space. It was a weird dance of colors, sonorous sounds, and smoke. Someone had lit space on fire. But there was something evil, something sinister about it. It caused her a great deal of anguish. She winced and writhed with the intensity of the whole experience.

Suddenly there was a thud, and she woke up. A vase had fallen from a small side table and crashed. Kubo realized she had fallen asleep on the couch. It was a winter night, and the temperature had dropped drastically after midnight. Her body shook and shivered with the cold. She felt her heart racing in her chest, hammering away.

And then, standing in that cold Six Nips night - it hit her. She had had a vision of some terrible travesty. But what was it? Maybe it was the alcohol or perhaps a nightmare brought on by her exhaustion. But then again, she remembered it vividly, with every minute and intricate detail. *How do I recall it so vividly if it was just a dream?* She wondered.

She thought for a while but failed to put her finger on it. Sitting on her bed, thinking about this she realized she hadn't checked her Sanbanak for several weeks. She decided to give it a go.

Kubo opened her sanbanak. There were several frantic messages from Akan and Uxa. A letter from Pop-Pop. Akan's messages kept hinting at some major incident, but as usual he had forgotten to provide any details. So, she decided to run the Aspa 1 program, one of the scores of horses she had built to scan the Milky Way. The scan did not show anything unusual for the first few minutes, but then it threw a flag at the X-Land H33 and the surrounding Kiboz system.

"Something's not right," Kubo murmured quietly as she ran several other programs to get to the root of this. She was absolutely shocked at what she saw.

"Oh my god!" She shouted as she looked at the screen. Aspa 1 had built a complete visual sequence of the attack that had destroyed the X-Land. With her image reconstruction algos, she was able to find out where the kill shot had come from and who had ordered it after cross referencing the name of the ship and its coordinates at the time.

This was big. Kubo had to do something about it. She hadn't informed anyone from the team when she left. It was a personal journey, and she wanted to keep it that way. But this was big – way too big for her to keep with herself.

She thought for a moment and then decided to speak with her buddies, Akan and Uxa, back home.

55

THE WIZARD IS BACK ONLINE

A Virtual Conference.

"Whoa, whoa, whoa!" Akan was excited, practically hopping up and down at his desk.

"Can you keep it down? I'm trying to work here." Uxa was clearly irked at him, tossing a loose ball of paper in his direction.

They were the only ones left on the team, with everyone else gone. Jebbmy had asked them to find anything about the kill shot they could lay their hands on.

"It's Kubo!" Akan shouted again, "She is calling me,"

"What's up Kubo, where are you? We've been going nuts trying to find you." He spoke hurriedly before she could say a word.

"I know, I know, Akan," she said, "I am sorry I was out of pocket. Do you have the boss with you?"

"The boss!" Akan exclaimed, "He is gone, Kubo. Managed to get himself fired last week."

"Fired! how – but – what happened?" Kubo was startled. *"Who can dare do such a thing – what with his friendship with Zxea!"* she said, only to herself.

"Yeah, it's a long story. You have to come here ASAP. We are in the soup here. President Jebbmy has given us a ton of work, and it's just the two of us." Akan replied.

"President Jebbmy! Wow - so Zxea is gone too!" Kubo said, "So much has happened while I was away. But hey, we can catch up on the gossip later; I need to send you something important. You must share it with the president ASAP."

By now, Uxa had joined in the conversation peering over Akan's shoulder at the screen, "I am hoping you found something pertaining to the X-Land. We've been scrambling to find any information we can."

"Yes, that's what this is about, but let me warn you guys, the images are disturbing."

"Sure thing Kubo, we got this. We've become responsible and all in recent weeks - if you haven't noticed already! But hey, you are a lifesaver, you know that right?" Akan said.

56

JEBBMY COMES THROUGH

The Capital District of CLAN, Northern Milky Way.

IT WAS AN IMPROMPTU media strumcast. Jebbmy had decided there was no time to spend butting heads with diplomates on this. *Let the universe know what has transpired. Things would fall into place soon after.* He had instructed himself.

"Dear citizens of the universe. Today, I speak to you not as a politician but as a fellow human. As you might have heard – the Milky Way galaxy has been pushed to the verges of a massive war. A war that no one wants, that no one needs. Today, as I say this, I hope that all of us, including me, come to our senses and do what is right."

"I want to address the issues at the center of this conflict. First, there was a mistake that happened on our side. One of our security programs accidentally entered the CERS's defenses. Naturally, the CERS considered this lapse an incursion – and an attack on their sovereignty. The second and the more severe issue, is the savage attack by an unknown entity that wiped out the X-Land H33 system."

"Today, here, now" – Jebbmy continued in an astute, unwavering voice. He had never been clearer about his actions as he was now. "I want to apologize to the people of the CERS. We are sorry; we made a mistake we shouldn't have made. But believe me, when I say this, the CLAN never had any intentions of starting a war with the CERS, or for that matter, with anyone within this beautiful universe of ours."

"As of this morning, we have received robust evidence pointing to some rogue elements within the Alpha Magnon galaxy,"

Jebbmy paused and slipped into contemplation. *I am making a big allegation here. There will be implications - but no price is bigger than achieving peace. I must do what needs to be done.*

Mheilia, who stood behind the Praxicam, waved at him, pushing him to move along.

"That they had, in fact," he continued, "Ordered the kill shot on the X-Land. It was a hit job carried out by the Drakevin Syndicate. The evidence is being made available for anyone to see as we speak."

"In light of this discovery, I want to appeal to the good people of the CERS. Let us talk. Let us sit together and work through our differences. This incredible galaxy has suffered too much – we have to end this madness now. We owe it to our people, our generations to come."

By the time the strumcast was over, the universal media was buzzing with wild speculations. Jebbmy expected this reaction, but he also knew he had dodged a bullet, at least for the foreseeable future.

57
A Reluctant Ceasefire
Planet K000-9, Neutral Zone 1.

Kiriptof and Pixi had finally managed to get the top brass in one meeting room.

President Jebbmy had arrived with Kiriptof and Mheilia, his chief of staff. Commander in chief Kimnabav was joined by Quapic, her operations chief, and Ambassador Pixi.

Ambassador Kiriptof played a good host and ordered the best Palpanese food possible and antique Napa Valley wines. The tension in the dome was clearly palpable. After more than a month of a tense standoff, both parties had agreed to discuss a potential ceasefire.

Kimnabav looked stern in her military chief uniform. Jebbmy looked disinterested, in a loose-fitting suite, but that was his usual expression. Kiriptof had specifically asked Pixi to ignore the look if they believed President Jebbmy appeared disinterested. "That is his twenty-four by seven look. Believe me, Ambassador, he desires this truce more than anyone else in the galaxy. The guy wants to retire and write poetry for Zumt's sake."

After everyone was seated comfortably, sipping expensive wine sponsored by the hapless taxpayers, they began the deliberations.

Ambassador Kiriptof spoke first. "Thank you all for coming here today. I am delighted to host such a dignified congregation." Kiriptof paused to clear his throat. "In the interest of maintaining peace and prosperity within our galaxy, I herewith propose an immediate bilateral ceasefire and a complete disengagement of forces along the frontiers," he looked at Jebbmy and Kimnabav sitting across from each other.

"I am good with this. We never wanted this war." Jebbmy said without looking at either Kiriptof or Kimnabav. He was trying to gander at the greenery through the massive glass walls.

Kimnabav shook her head in disbelief, "Your actions, honorable President, betray the opposite message, if I may say so."

"Kvazim Chief," Kiriptof said, "We have already issued an unconditional apology to the people of the CERS. We now ask you to let bygones be bygones."

"Kvazim Kimnabav, a conflict by definition means two parties are involved in it." Jebbmy did not mince his words. "We have ignored several such attempts from your side in the past."

"Be that as it may," Kimnabav retorted, "This whole thing started with your incursion, which makes you the aggressor. I believe we are on the receiving end of aggression here, honorable President."

"We both know that is not true, Kvazim Chief," Jebbmy replied as he put his vintage wine chalice down. "But we want to move past any bitterness now. What do you want?"

Ambassador Pixi, who had been silent, said, "I have given a list of our demands to Ambassador Kiriptof here, honorable President."

"Can you summarize, Ambassador?" Kimnabav shot an unpleasant look at Pixi.

"Yes, Kvazim. The people of CERS would like to stake a claim at three X-Lands in the neutral region 4 for research purposes."

Mheilia could not resist jumping in, "We can make a concession and give two. Three is out of the question."

Pixi looked at Kimnabav, who nodded in agreement. "Fine. But we need absolute control over the X-lands," said Pixi.

"We can work with that." Mheilia replied before the president. Jebbmy half tilted his head, indicating his agreement.

Ambassador Pixi then went on with a few more trade demands. Mheilia negotiated hard with him, but it was a quick agreement in the end.

"Isn't this wonderful, Ambassador Pixi?" Said Kiriptof.

"Wonderful indeed, Ambassador Kiriptof. We can all shake hands now and enjoy the delicacies!" Pixi replied.

58

A Fickle Thing Called Love

The Capital District of CLAN, Northern Milky Way.

"Hey, listen, I am sorry about last time." It was Marxzib on Zxea's Vabaka. It'd been a month since he was fired.

"I understand, bighead" She replied with a smile, as she looked at him. His head looked bigger on the zereal screen. It looked like he had finally shaved and taken a bath.

"What have you been up to?" he asked.

"Nothing. I went to the beach. Spent a month there."

"Alone?"

"Of course, alone. Wanted to clear my head."

"You could have called me."

"I tried, remember?"

"Yeah, I am sorry about that. I guess I did not take that thing well."

"If you mean wallowing in sheer, tubs of ice cream and doughnuts - I guess we can say that." She said impishly.

He laughed. "Yeah, I am emotional like that."

"So, what's next for you?"

"Nothing. I guess I will be taking this year. Take that sabbatical I dreamt about forever."

"Nice. I guess I am on a sabbatical too." She replied.

"Ahem." Marxzib cleared his throat. He cracked his knuckles. Then he started playing with his nose.

"Get on with it, Marxzib. I am not going to be single forever." Zxea threw her hands in the air in exasperation.

"Well. Umm. Thank you. I mean. What I wanted to say is, why not spend this sabbatical in question together? If you are up for it."

"I am up for anything. Did you have a place in mind?"

"Somewhere far from here. Away from all this animosity."

"I'd love that. Are you thinking neutral zones?"

"Yes. Chandrama. I have heard a lot about the place."

"Fine. Pack your bags, Marxzib. Pick me up in about an hour."

"Yes!" He threw his fists in the air.

Part Five

Picking up the Pieces

59

THE HORRORS OF WAR

An Independent Media Organization, Planet Chandrama, Neutral Zone 2.

"THE DESTRUCTION IS MASSIVE," Zipwe spoke solemnly.

Never in his long life of ninety-one years had he thought a day like this would come. A great catastrophe had happened.

A popular quantum stream channel had invited the veteran show host to run a special on the destruction of the H 33 and the Kiboz system. Retired some three decades ago from active journalism, Koper Zipwe was nothing short of a legend in the field. He preferred to stay alone on a remote X-Land, but when he heard of this travesty, he knew it was his time to speak up.

"Historians," he continued in a sad, deep voice, "Have considered the lives lost; the properties damaged. The birds, trees, and animals that were made extinct."

Grim pictures flashed on screens across galaxies. People watched in shock as the images flooded their Praximas from multiple sources. Many cried. Several prayed. Spirituality had made a comeback in the wake of the tragedy.

"One estimate says about a million people died when the planet's system collapsed. The debris will take several decades to settle down in space. There is talk of evacuating some colonies in the adjacent planet systems to avoid collisions with the remnants floating in space."

Zipwe continued in his calm voice that shook a little every now and then.

"Some commentators have blamed the CLAN for having a clandestine base. There was always a risk of massive-scale blasts and radiation with the amount of radioactive material stored on the planet. The people working there were practically sitting on a ticking time bomb."

"But is it fair for us to judge anyone involved? The research staff working on X-Land H33 had assumed this risk when they had signed up for the jobs. It was an opportunity to do important research. Many spent good decades of their lives on the X-Land, away from their families."

"Some also feel the aftereffects of radiation exposure could have been horrific in case of partial destruction of the system – it was good in a way that nothing was left. But these are all mourners' morbid theories. Lives were lost for no reason. Families were damaged and broken forever."

"Come to think of it, whose war is it really? None of the people involved seem to have achieved much. A young and dynamic leader like Zxea had to resign from her job. Senator Jebbmy Nikpoa reluctantly became the president of the CLAN, but he does not seem very keen on it. Some lobbyists say he wants to go into the shadows quietly now. He believes he has achieved enough, and it is time to pass the baton."

"Chief Ukama had to resign in embarrassment over the mining scandal. He left as a sad man with a tarnished legacy. Chief Kimnabav, who allegedly colluded with rogue elements from the CLAN in removing chief Ukama, leads a very unstable coalition at the helm, with an uncertain future. The leaders of the syndicate are now wanted war criminals with bounties on their heads."

"Marxzib, the analyst caught in the middle of this fiasco, lost his career and his marriage. Though he is rumored to have left the capital with ex-President Zxea, not much is known about what became of him other than rumor."

"But no one has suffered as much as those who lost their lives. Innocent victims of power, ambition, and endless greed. There are no winners in a war - there never were any winners in any war. Some people like to believe that wars bring about reforms - but let us talk proportions here. What is the cost of human capital? Can the lost lives be replaced? The talent, the positivity and the hope that was annihilated? Who knows what they would have achieved otherwise - had they been given a chance at living a full, natural life? We will never know what greatness these individuals would have attained."

"Humans have been bestowed with free will - but does it allow us to be the judges to decide who lives and who doesn't? What could possibly justify the death of thousands of children in war? What of those who were sick and frail - were they even given a chance to run for their lives? An optimist may say it will all come good in the end if you consider the larger scheme of things, but I fail to see what good can come out of this moment of chaos. I am not religious, and I sure, as Zumt, do not want to bother you with theological debates, but we must discuss the immorality of war."

"Albert Einstein, our great ancestor, asked us to give up war some four thousand years ago. He had asked us to *employ our powers of reason to settle disputes* instead. But what have we done since then? The spread of nuclear armaments has flourished century after century after century."

"My heart," concluded Zipwe, "Goes out to the trees and the animals that perished in this senseless travesty. The sacred mountains that passed, the glorious rivers that dried. All creation sullied at human hands. Tonight, I sign off with a heavy heart and ask you all to pray for all that was lost. I wish you all peace."

60
A New Dawn

The People's Nation of Priscia, Neutral Zone 4.

Priscia shone bright, resembling festive nights from the Earthen Age. The streets were adorned with lights and festive decorations. In accordance with Priscian customs, there were restrictions on the use of technology. Those invited were asked to arrive two days before the celebration and to travel using traditional space routes rather than relying on their Sanbahaks. This allowed for early festivities and ample time to adjust to the effects of space travel.

Today marked the inauguration of the third front - though people preferred to call it the third conglomerate.

Almost a third of the Milky Way constituents had opted to be a part of the Non-Aligned Milky Way front, also known as the NAMY. Most of the autonomous planetary states favored the proposal when the Riok first introduced it. A small number had expressed fears about the rigid Priscian traditions transcending into the alliance. They were concerned that the front would naturally provide Priscia with a dominant position and potentially limit progress in the fields of science and technology. Nevertheless, the Riok was able to alleviate these concerns with his calm and effective arguments. It was decided that the third front would not follow the Priscian customs and would stay abreast with contemporary science and tech. Those who wanted to follow the Priscian way were free to do so. In practice, except for some returning

Priscian expatriates, no one else had opted to follow it for obvious reasons. The Priscian way denounced creature comforts and at times promoted rigorous physical effort. This lifestyle was too difficult for the majority, accustomed to the technological conveniences and creature comforts of the era.

***

A large assembly was convened in the central court of the Priscian capital. Following the initial introductions, representatives from various planets delivered their speeches. Most speeches were pompous and drab, except for Kqinpim Mzxuko's brief but splendid monologue.

"My Milky Way brothers and sisters!" She had started among thunderous applause.

"It is a great honor for me to join this alliance, underlining our commitment to the principles of non-alignment. We refuse to allow the Milky Way galaxy, our magnificent home, to be held hostage by two dominant forces. Our galaxy has been plundered and pillaged by operatives from both sides. Several planets and X-Lands have been ruined due to the excessive extraction of precious elements. Many Qanets are now uninhabitable and numerous others are doomed to suffer a slow and painful death. The conglomerate leaders have become wealthier, but their people still suffer. The fruits from the progress achieved haven't been distributed equally."

"Shame! Shame!" Cries erupted from the crowd.

"Is this the kind of future we desire for future generations? Isn't this a flagrant violation of the principles and the values that the galactic civilization's founders established?"

Another thunderous round of applause rose from the crowd. The response Kqinpim received from the crowd was making many leaders nervous.

"It is our responsibility to uphold and defend the commoner's interest in the Milky Way of the future," Kqinpim added. "All civilians should have unlimited, unfettered access to modern technology and education. Planetary mining must be banned entirely for the next 50 years, and most importantly," she paused before taking a big breath, "The perpetrators must be investigated and held accountable for the pillaging they have done."

"Aye! Aye!" The atmosphere was filled with excitement and exuberance as the public was on the brink of communal euphoria commonly experienced at such large gatherings. Many were attending a public meeting for the first time in their lives.

"Therefore, my comrades," she proceeded, speaking even more loudly, striking her fists on the vintage lectern in front of her, "We demand justice for the Milky Way, here and now!"

Her voice drowned out in the crowd's thunderous applause and appreciative hurrahs.

Clearly, a new political leader was born.

The Riok was not completely surprised by this outcome. He knew well that if there was a void, people would come up and fill it. He monitored the faces of the other leaders as Kqinpim spoke. She had literally snatched the leadership baton and made it her own.

One of the critical agenda items for the assembly was to select a leader, preferably unanimously. Many had arrived ready to vie for the position. No one had expected a relatively young leader from an obscure planet to come and upstage everyone.

Aeqima silently observed the proceedings from her seat in a secluded corner. She preferred to stay away from the limelight. People from all over the galaxy had gathered in Priscia, and there existed a great deal of interest in her as the mastermind behind the Priscia operations for the past three decades. Reporters and fans had been pursuing her for the past few days, making it difficult for her to escape their attention. Between looking after the arrangements for the assembly and avoiding the paps, she had yet to get any time to converse with the Riok. This troubled her. She wanted to know if Kinmuk contemplated taking on a leadership role. The Priscian customs definitely did not allow this. This was a unique situation for both of them. Kinmuk was treading a thin line between asserting the importance of the Priscian way of life and yet staying off the power that would have come with such an assertion. Aeqima knew well that this balance took a lot of work to achieve – and could easily take a toll on his mind. She did not want to lose Kinmuk; she hadn't worked with a better Riok than him.

The formation of this alliance presented a big opportunity for the Riok. As a Priscian master, he had trained hard to abstain from desire and ambition. The principles of leading a simple life, free of greed formed the basis of the Priscian state. When Pihimay Veyo, the state's founding mother, imagined the free land, she had envisioned it free of human frailties. She lived the lonely life of a minimalist monk following the principles of detachment. She had no master as such. According to the legend, she had found her own way, one day meditating under a Peepal tree on an abandoned colony on Earth. It is said that there were only four individuals present on Earth during that time, in its four corners, all engaged in meditation and seeking their own paths. The Earth had been abandoned for over two million years now and had yet to become a novelty tourist hub. There, all four became great spiritual leaders, eventually with a great following.

Pihimay, only twenty-seven back then, returned to the world with a vision, a thought. She scouted the universe with three of her disciples and finally chose this one pristine X-Land, un-inhabited, unadulterated by any human presence up until then.

There, she had found Priscia, the land of the free. And to this day, the Priscians followed her teachings, albeit within worldly bounds.

When Kinmuk took the reins over from Lme Kso, people already knew him as a wise young man of a meditative frame. A voracious reader and a talented essayist, he had four books of his own by the age of twenty-seven. Many believed him fit to become the next Riok when the time came.

His time had come early, when Lme Kso decided to retire a year before his term ended, citing an intense yearning to meditate and explore his mind further. His abdication had caused quite a turmoil in the land. The council of the elders had found merit in Lme's claims and allowed him an honorable exit. That meant the reins came over to Kinmuk, still in his early thirties.

"Did I give away too much?" This one question had been bothering him a great deal during the ceremony. Amid the excitement, the flair, and the revelry around him, Kinmuk cut a detached figure. He felt a great turmoil churning in his head.

Thoughts clouded his mind as one speaker took the stage after the other.

"What is the root of human ambition? Wasn't it my ambition that made me sit in this chair? Is the Riok truly free from desire? Why would a state like Priscia need a head, a leader, or a master? Why would a monk desire to become the head of monks - isn't that an act of ambition in itself? How many times have I drifted - countless and did penances after that? Like when I became attracted to a Priscian woman, a writer who had come to seek my guidance. I saw the spark, the hunger for knowing the truth in her eyes. What had pulled me to her? Her

physical beauty, her striking appearance? Her beautiful eyes, her lips, her youthful contours? The way she spoke, smiled? Or just her intelligence?"

The Rioks were meant to suffer in their agonies alone, which Kinmuk did after this episode. Aeqima had guessed his predicament. He had seen the look on Aeqima's face when he had announced heading into meditation for several weeks without food, water, and human contact. And what had this penance achieved? Kinmuk thought, *"Didn't I escape from it because of my extreme hunger - that I, the spiritual master of the Priscians, could not conquer?"*

"People believe in the absolute miracles of spiritual leaders - no, they want to believe in them. This urge to believe, to know that there is someone among us, a direct conduit to the supreme power, creates spiritual middlemen and women; and then a living being is revered, despite the knowledge that humans, by design, are fallible. Earlier today, they worshiped me as the messenger of God. But am I the one? Am I not tempted today, in this assembly, to make an evocative speech and become the leader of the third front? Isn't this an outcome of my efforts that the people of this galaxy have started looking for options? As a human, do I get to taste the sweet fruits of my labor - or is that amoral for the Riok, the beloved master of Priscian people? I have given up all desires – but have I indeed?"

"And if I do it, I commit myself to this ambition, would the Priscian state fall, finally? I am sure some people would love to see that happen. Priscia has had her share of adversaries over all these years. There were countless critiques written against the Priscian way. Some even blamed us for sabotaging our own progress. Many called us unscientific and superstitious. Prisicia's detractors want to see her fail. What if this fall is brought down by the most beloved Priscian himself?"

His contemplation was interrupted by another raucous round of applause from the crowd in anticipation of the next speaker. It was the flamboyant Sazmin Trundr. Sazmin represented the planet Cuma, which housed a large and prosperous civilization.

"Howdy, everybody!" Sazmin got the crowd moving from the minute he started speaking Sazmin definitely knew how to please the crowd. For the next ten minutes, he cajoled and enthralled the audience. In the end, he evoked lines from Tennyson, a vintage poet from the Earthen Age. The poem read something like this:

"Tho much is taken, much abides; and tho"
We are not now that strength which in old days
Moved Earth and heaven, that which we are, we are;
One equal temper of heroic hearts,
Made weak by time and fate, but strong in will
To strive, to seek, to find, and not to yield."

By now, it became clear that there would be two contenders - three depending on what the Riok decided, in the ring to lead the NAMY.

The assembly headed to a close, and the air was thick with anticipation regarding what the Riok was going to say.

Naturally, when he stood up to speak, applause rose from all corners.

The Riok donned a pale blue robe made from homespun fabric. It exuded the minimalism one would expect from a monk.

"Fellow comrades, I welcome you once more to this land of the free."

He did not have the baritone voice Sazmin had or the graceful personality of Kqinpim. What he had, though, was a comforting voice, one that would soothe bleeding hearts.

"Mother Phimay Veyo laid the foundation of this land eight hundred years ago. Her vision, to build a space that welcomed anyone and everyone who wanted to contribute to staying in peace. To live and let others live. Our constitution asks us to treat the universe as a family. And in a family, there is no place for hatred, for vendetta. For revenge."

"When I had appealed to the great leaders from this beautiful place we call home, our Milky Way galaxy- my intentions were to unite this small part of the universe, so there are no wars, and our younger ones can still have a great future. A future that is one to all - that does not discriminate, that abhors violence. We do not want the mighty federations to dictate how people live their lives. Humans are birthed for a purpose, and it's everyone's prerogative that they find their cause, their very own *nibbanas*."

"In that, I see no place for violence. Throughout the history of the human race, we have seen enough bloodshed and massacres. It is time we undertake conscious efforts to achieve peace. I know the world does not work the way a Monk like me would want it to. But as thinking and well-meaning beings, we must try our best to balance perspectives."

"And that, my friends, is the idea behind this alliance, this friendship. We want to balance the power dynamic within this galaxy. This alliance is, indeed, a new dawn, a new beginning in the history of the Milky Way. As the planets move in their assigned circles, stars shine, and rivers flow, we, here in the land of the free, begin this new order, a new path toward peace, justice, and harmony."

The Riok's words were met with applause each time he took a pause.

"Priscians," he continued, "Do not aspire to achieve power. We do not intend to use this phenomenon for our benefit. The Priscian way does not allow us to fall prey to covetousness or ambition. We will only serve as catalysts in this great human experiment."

"Therefore, my friends, as the convener of this front, I want you all to choose a leader and a council of doers to run the matters of day-to-day importance for this alliance. Tomorrow, we will hold, with your permission," he looked at the leaders around him, "The election for the leader and council of doers. As you cast your votes, I urge you to put the people's interest before anything else."

"Thank you once again! I wish peace and prosperity to you all."

The Riok raised his hands high in the air and looked at the sky for a moment. Then, he brought his palms together in the *Anjali Mudra* and bowed to the assembly.

Postscript

Now that you have read this entire story, I assume you are wondering what became of the people involved. Well, I would not be able to tell you all about everyone right away, but let me end the tale here, for now, on a positive note.

Yours truly,
Minco Turex

***

The *Wreckers*, Planet Chandrama. Neutral Zone 2.

Xules and Kwaqa had gone to the *Wreckers* for a dinner. Kwaqa had secured a job on Planet Ilna, so Xules decided to give her a going away treat. Kwaqa noticed Xules kept observing a couple seated a few tables away.

"Do you know them, Mr. Kampert?" She asked Xules.

"Yeah, I most certainly do. It's Zxea Qollins. And with her is our man Marxzib."

"Really?" Kwaqa's eyes widened with surprise. "Wow," she said. "I am a big fan of hers. Do you think I can go and - talk to her?"

"Knock yourself out!" Xules replied.

Kwaqa quietly got up and went over to the table Zxea was sitting at.

"Umm. Excuse me," she played with the zip of her jacket as she stood awkwardly at the table. Her words got lost in the hubbub of the place, but thankfully, Zxea noticed her.

"What do you want, young lady?" Zxea asked.

"Hello. I mean, good evening. I am Kwaqa. A big fan of yours, I wanted to come and say hi, nothing more." A big smile appeared on Kwaqa's face.

"Well, hello to you. I am glad you came over!" Zxea said. Judging by the number of bottles on her table, she looked to be in a good mood.

"So where is your boss? Is he here with you?" Marxzib said.

"Yes, Mr. Lumik. I am happy to meet you too. I have heard a lot about you and your team."

"Umm. I guess we have become famous lately."

"Who's her boss?" It was now Zxea's turn to ask a question. "And how do you know her?"

"I used to be a spy, remember?" Marxzib smiled sheepishly.

"Our young friend here," he pointed at Kwaqa and said, "Is a protege of Xules, the infamous."

Zxea raised an eyebrow, but for a second only. Then she said, "Well, Ok. Everybody has to work someplace, I guess."

"Mr. Kampert is right over there. Should I call him?" Kwaqa returned to her usual cheerfulness. Her cheeks had turned red and there was a sparkle in her voice.

"Maybe not," Marxzib was quick to refuse, "We are not on talking terms exactly."

"What?" Zxea said, waving both her hands before him. "How do you know him?"

"I have known Xules for a long time. We went to school together."

"Wow, anything else I should know about?" Zxea said with a hint of amusement in her voice.

"Come on, Zxea. You're being dramatic. I cannot possibly tell you about every person I grew up with."

"You suck at being coy, Marxzib." She replied. "I think this was important enough for me to know."

"I am so sorry," Kwaqa realized she had inadvertently made the couple quarrel. "I shouldn't have crashed your table like this. I apologize."

She turned on her heels and started to leave.

"No, wait," Zxea stopped her. "Pull up a chair, and don't worry, we are fine."

"Yeah, we like bickering," Marxzib grinned as he added. "Why don't you invite Xules over here as well? Maybe I do want to talk to him."

Kwaqa pulled a chair and waved at Xules, who seemed all geared up to join them.

"So, how do you know Xules?" Zxea asked.

"Mr. Kampert was best friends with my late father. He is practically the only family I have left," Kwaqa replied without realizing she had teared up.

"I am so sorry," Zxea said as she put a hand on Kwaqa's cheek. "Believe me, I understand. If it's some consolation, I grew up without a father. I have no extended family either."

Kwaqa smiled uneasily.

Xules pulled up a chair for himself, "Well, well, well!" He chuckled as he sprawled in the chair. "Look what the Zumt dragged into *Wreckers* today. Lucky us, aren't we, dear Kwaqa?" He half bowed to Zxea and said, "Kvazim ex-President," then turning to Marxzib, "Mr. Ex spy, or shall I say ex-friend."

"Hello to you as well, conman in chief," Marxzib remarked, "Order whatever you would like to - now that you have made yourself comfortable here."

Zxea laughed. She was enjoying this surprise meet. "It's interesting to see you in person, Xules. Believe me - you are a popular name in political circles."

Zxea continued to be cheerful. Kwaqa thought it was the effect of the festive atmosphere around them.

"Well, I try," Xules replied with a broad grin.

"So, what brings you here, Xules?" Marxzib asked.

"Same thing as you," Xules replied, with a slight wink.

"What is that supposed to mean? We are not outlaws," Marxzib snapped.

"But you are - what is that term again - ah yes, pariahs! And Chandrama has a place for everyone - outlaws, pariahs, mavericks, and geniuses." Xules made conducting motions with his hands, like a concertmaster.

"Ok, you make a good point, Xules," Zxea said as she turned to Kwaqa. "But I want to know more about you, Kwaqa. Aren't you studying somewhere?"

"Not at the moment, but I will be starting at Spacemart soon. Mr. Kampert called in a favor."

"Well, if I were you, I would definitely go to the university, you know - study for a few years before joining the workforce."

"I don't know. Honestly, I am not sure what I want to do with my life yet," Kwaqa said, tapping her fingers on the table.

"Well," Zxea continued, "I am guessing you have a good eye for politics. The Academy of Political Sciences could be a good place for you. I can put in a word if you want. Still have some good friends there."

Kwaqa did not know how to respond to this. She was overwhelmed by this kind gesture from Zxea, whom she had met only for a few minutes. She looked at Xules.

"I am afraid the ex-president makes a valid argument here, dear Kwaqa. I think you should take her up on her word. Do not worry about me. You can come and visit me anytime. It's not like I am a fugitive. Well, technically, I am, but not here anyways."

Kwaqa noticed a tenderness in Xules eyes even as he tried to joke about it. She did not know how to respond. Xules had been a father figure to her.

"I am disappointed, man," Marxzib said, disturbing the uneasy silence. "I know you are in bed with the Syndicate, Xules, and look at what they did. Don't you feel remorse?" He looked at Xules with probing eyes.

"You remind me of an old religious saying, my ex-friend." Xules was back in his element. "Do not throweth a stone unless you knoweth you haven't sinned or something on those lines. But you get my drift, don't you?" Xules raised his eyebrows and his glass of whiskey. "And talking of remorse, many people actually," he took a dramatic pause, "Hold you," he pointed at Marxzib, "Responsible for this mess, in case you haven't heard."

Marxzib threw his hands in the air. "What audacity! Don't try to pin this on me now, man."

"I only played my role. Isn't that something we all do?" Xules said. "And honestly, I had no idea the Syndicate was in cahoots with the Magnonians. I am only a small cog in this big bad machine. But," he stopped for a moment. "I am in no hurry to proclaim which way the pendulum of morality swings either. You call me a conman, but I say this universe is the biggest con job ever." Xules opened his hands wide, trying to take stock of the world around him.

"It's a sham, to be honest. So please don't blame me. Well, at least, I don't blame me. Never."

"I know you don't," Marxzib scoffed.

Kwaqa looked amused. She was observing the three as they made their arguments. She wanted to speak but then thought otherwise.

By now the usuals had flocked to the middle and started singing an old-world sea shanty. Xules got out of his chair and joined them in the singing.

> *Where am I to go, me buddies? Where am I to go?*
>
> *For I am a young spaceman buddies, where am I to go?*
>
> *I've seen a thousand ships go down, where am I to go?*

*And there's no takers for the
glory, where am I to go?*

*Yo hi-dy hi-dy hi-dy hi-dy
hi-dy hi-dy hi-dy yo !*

*Where am I to go me bud-
dies ? Where am I to go?**

The conjoined sounds of their singing were enhanced by the sizable dome-like ceiling of the *Wreckers*. The alcohol-laden bonhomie of the chorus had spun off some misty magic in the air. For a moment Kwaqa felt like they were singing her own song. She wondered where life would take her now. The wonderful people she would meet. The beautiful wonders of life she would see.

Soon, the song ended, and she realized she should get going.

"Thank you for your time, Kvazim," she got up to leave. "It was wonderful spending time with you today."

"Pleasure, Kwaqa. I wish you well. Think about what I said. Don't throw away your life." Zxea replied, her voice full of compassion.

Kwaqa shook hands with Zxea and Marxzib and took their leave. She had a new spark in her eyes, a bright hope. And hope, is a good old thing.

**This song is inspired by "Where am I to go M'Johnnie's," a traditional sea shanty*

Social Media

Like this book? Let me know!

Drop me an e-mail:
anantdhavale@gmail.com

Follow me on Facebook @ Anant Dhavale

Find me on Instagram @anant_ad2

Check out my Blog:
https://newagepoems.blogspot.com/

Appendices

Characters and Entities

The CLAN:
CLAN - Conglomerate of planets and other entities in the northern part of the Milky Way galaxy.

The politicians:
Zxea Qollins – President of the CLAN.

Jebbmy Nikpoa - Trusted parliamentarian and senior leader from the CLAN.

Leqo and Kaman - Opportunistic politicians, friends of Jebbmy.

Ghirnot Ceeth – Zxea's principal opponent and archenemy.

President Zxea's staff members:
Zebero - Political adviser to President Zxea, and a friend of Marxzib's.

Mheilia - Parliamentary affairs minister in President Zea's ministry.

Kamado - Chief of staff to Zxea.

Jeno - Legal representative for President Zxea.

Senator Ghirnot's staff:
Chaliza – Ghirnot's personal assistant and closest aid.

Kixmado - IT Intelligence head for Ghirnot's ministry.

Counselor Chia - Ghirnot's lawyer.

Analysts (Also known as spies):

Marxzib Lumik– hacker, sleuth, friend, and possible romantic interest of President Zxea.

Akan – Youngest member on Marxzib's team.

Uxa – Marb's assistant manager.

Kubo – A bright young analyst who works with Marxzib.

Qleqo – Marxzib's wife.

Peber – Analyst in Marxzib's team, he breaks away from the operation and betrays Marxzib. Has anger issues.

Kubo's family and friends:

Wajko Pulo - Kubo's foster dad.

Oip Mklan - Wajko's friend. A maverick and a psychic.

Ugoz - Kubo's boyfriend.

Ksopaj and Duxo – Kubo's buddies.

Sixo – The elderly inn keeper from Kaxoules.

Military generals and others:

Hermip Iyo - Chief of the CLAN's Spatial Security Force.

General Zima - Head of the CLAN's nuclear arsenal.

Niho Kiriptof - the Ambassador of the CLAN to the CERS.

The CERS:

CERS - Conglomerate of planets and other entities in the northern part of the Milky Way.

Key players:

Chief Ukama - Commander in chief of the CERS.

Kimnabav Yejino - Ukama's deputy and first in command.

Senator Jity – Senator and political adviser to Chief Ukama.

Feliv Hioma - Political adviser to Chief Ukama.

Chief Lieutenant Lopki - An officer with the CERS.

General Nodfi - A high-ranking general with the CERS.

General Dulerty - Commander of the Aviation Council for CERS. A liberal individual with friends in the CERS.

Rikey - Dulerty's confidant and political heir.

Ambassador Pixi – Ambassador of the CERS to the CLAN.

Uxcy Civorxta: Head of The Torial party.

Waqipk - A key member of the Cabal, the sane one.

Kiquib, Nibkowt - Other members of the Cabal.

Kitgobx – Chief Ukama's son in law.

Thexacorp - A rogue drilling firm with a bad reputation for ruining planets and X-Lands.

Independent players:

Xules Kampert– A small-time underground operator working with rogue elements in the CERS and the CLAN.

Kwaqa - Xules's closest aid.

The Drakevin Syndicate:

Pwesdra Hok – A key business operative, leads the heavy metals business.

Ohuima Yej - Pwesdra's partner, political lobbyist.

Chief Gydsa - Leader of the syndicate.

Crew of the mercenary ship Hawk 1A

Captain Aqwza: Captain of the ship Hawk 1A.

Officer Luikip – Second officer.

Officer Zoxzi – Another officer.

The Priscians:

Priscia - An independent nation that refuses to merge with either of the conglomerates. Proponents of galactic non-alignment.

Riok - Head of an independent planet nation Priscia. Riok is a ceremonial position, a new Riok is chosen every five years. Retired

Rioks must migrate to an unknown location, only to come back only in unprecedented circumstances.

Aeqima - Principal advisor to the Riok.

Pihimay Veyo - Founding mother of the Priscian nation.

Kinmuk Wey - The prevailing Riok.

The Wreckers:

The Wreckers: An extremely popular pub on Planet Chandrama.

Pidbitzo – A patron, popular with the usuals.

Duboxzi - Pidbitzo's friend.

Bimaxzi – Manager and server at the Wreckers.

These characters appear only to show the people's reactions to war.

The media, independent activists and analysts:

Rtuolip - A popular strumcast host.

Kideii - A popular tv journalist.

Riffplo - Kideii's partner.

Zipwe - A widely respected elderly show host.

Blixipi - Noted environmental activist.

Colonel Movsy - A retired army colonel turned defense analyst.

Planet K000-9. - An isolated remote planet in a far corner of the Milky Way. It lies in neutral territory. Preferred destination for clandestine meetings. It lies uninhabited except for stray visitors.

Planet Chandrama – A beautiful planet in the neutral zone, known as the cultural paradise of the modern world.

Some Concepts

Vabaka- A ubiquitous conductor chip-particle built into people's memories; built from rare materials found in asteroid remnants. Migbodium, to be precise. It can clear matter, including human tissues, and connect with any device nearby for information transfer.

Boxqui audits – Financial audits run by the CLAN. These are highly random and clandestine.

Sanbanak - A machine that evolved from twentieth-century computers.

Sanbahak - Preferred mode of transportation in the seventh millennium.

Cosmic Death - Most diseases were conquered, and people rarely died of natural causes in the seventh millennium. However, a phenomenon emerged where people died due to cosmic aberrations sucking life out of them. This is how most people died during the time of the story.

During the phenomenon's early days, people blamed everyone, ranging from governments to space travel companies to food organizations. Later day discoveries established it as a natural evolution process meant to control the human population.

Some believed it emerged as nature's reaction to humans breaching the time and space continuum.

Supernova B1 boundary – The border between the CERS and the CLAN.

Quantixos - Something like a trillion.

Xozilamide Acetate - A drug used to relieve space lag.

The Earthen Age: Human era until the end of the 29th century AD.

Galactalism: A trait similar to nationalism from the Earthen Age.

Praxima – A visual representation of data. Everyone carries a Praxima, largely made of an algorithm that can be projected on any surface from the mind.

Zumt – There is no hell or heaven in the seventh millennium. Everything beyond explanation is simply, Zumt.

The Legal Panel – There is no judge in the judicial system for the CLAN. Instead, there is an intelligence algorithm called the Legal. The panel evaluates evidence and provides a guilty vs. not-guilty verdict. A jury has to either accept or decline the panel's ruling.

The CLAN House: CLAN constituents select representatives known as senators. Senators, in turn, choose a President who runs the government with the help of ministers.

The CERS Assembly: The citizens of the CERS select representatives, also known as senators, who choose a commander in chief. The Chief runs the government with a council of ministers.

Faraway galaxies: With the attenuation of space, no place can be considered to be truly far. However, there are health risks associated with longer travels, a cosmic death being one of them.

Kvazim – The word "Madam" was ruled to be offensive and banned from the political lexicon. Kvazim became the term of choice instead.

TV: The television has managed to survive, albeit in an evolved form, aided with state-of-the-art technology.

Sheer: A type of alcoholic beverage, best served cold.

Made in the USA
Middletown, DE
29 September 2024